The Return of the Six-Gunner

A Cole Decker Western

Van Holt

CHAPTER 1

Cole Decker entered the small restaurant with his black hat tilted low over his sharp gray eyes and his black coat pushed back away from his stag-handled Colt .45. The coat was unbuttoned over a tan shirt and his light brown pants weren't much darker than the shirt. He was a tall, lean, tough-looking man a little past thirty.

Five tough-looking men and a wild-looking girl in her late teens sat at the counter with their backs to the door. The girl's dark hair was cut short and she wore jeans, a man's shirt, and a gun in a holster on her shapely hip, but no hat.

The tall young woman standing behind the counter also wore jeans and had an even better figure than the girl. She had big dark eyes and glossy black hair. She wore no hat or gun, but Cole Decker had seen her wearing both.

Her eyes glowed when she looked past the six people sitting at the counter. "I didn't know you were still around."

"I've been riding around the country a little. Thought I'd stop by and see if you were still here."

"I don't know how much longer I'll be here," the beautiful dark girl known as Hoola said. "I'm gettin' kinda bored and restless."

"I figured you would," Cole Decker said quietly, keeping his clear gray eyes on Hoola and pretending not to notice that the six strangers sitting at the counter had turned their heads and were staring at him.

"I'll be damned!" said the boy at the far end of the counter. He didn't look much older than the girl. He had dark hair and eyes like the others, but his downy little mustache was almost blond. "I been readin' some of them dime novels, but I never thought I'd ever see a dime novel hero in the flesh. They usually take their guns off at the first sign of trouble and say, 'No guns. We can settle this with our fists.'"

Sitting beside the boy was a stout man who looked old enough to be his father. His thick mustache was black, but his beard was streaked with gray. His eyes were black and watchful and his voice sounded cautious and a little worried. "Take it easy, Tip. He don't look like no dime novel hero to me."

"You just ain't read enough of them dime novels to recognize the type, Mack," Tip said, getting to his feet and facing Decker. "Don't worry. Soon as I reach for my gun, he'll throw up his gun hand and yell, 'No guns. We'll settle this with out fists.' Wait and see."

Mack watched Decker with hard, scornful black eyes and said nothing more. Apparently Tip had convinced him that he knew what he was talking about.

Decker was aware that everyone in the room—including Hoola—was watching him to see what he would do. But he kept his bleak eyes on the boy and said nothing. He knew that any attempt to talk the boy out of a fight would only convince him that he had been right all along: Decker was afraid to fight him with guns.

Tip wore a short jacket that would not get in his way. His dark eyes were bright with excitement and sadistic amusement as he watched Decker. He seemed convinced that the tall sad-looking man would beg for his life when Tip's hand slapped the butt of his gun. Decker watched Tip's hand in somber silence and did not move.

Surprised and annoyed, Tip quit smiling and his dark eyes glinted as though to say, "I'll show that tall stupid greenhorn."

The next time Tip's hand slapped the butt of his gun, he pulled the gun from the holster and was raising it to take aim at the strip of tan showing under Decker's unbuttoned coat when something went horribly wrong. A gleaming gun roared in the tall man's hand and Tip spun around and hit the floor on his face. He lay motionless.

The other dark-haired, dark-eyed people sitting on stools at the counter stared at the dead boy with shocked eyes. Mack's hairy mouth hung open. The one with the twisted face and silly grin stopped grinning but showed no particular regret. The tough faces of the other two men were blank with surprise. One of them was stout and looked a lot like Mack. The other one was younger and taller.

It was the lean but shapely girl in jeans who jumped to her feet fumbling for her holstered gun and yelled at Cole Decker, "You're dead, mister!"

Decker cocked his gun and pointed it directly at her. The girl froze with her own gun only half drawn. Decker said in a harsh, angry voice, "The time for you to talk was before this happened. That goes for the rest of you. All of you just sat there and waited to see what I would do. You just saw what I would do. I'll tell you what I'm going to do if anybody else reaches for a gun. I'm going to start shooting and I may not stop till most of you are dead."

He looked directly at the girl and said, "I don't want to shoot a pretty girl, but I'm not going to stand here and let you shoot me. If you want to get any older, you better get your hand away from that gun, unbuckle your gun belt and drop it on the floor. That goes for all of you."

The girl stared at Decker's frozen gray eyes and didn't move.

The one called Mack said in a choked voice as he stood up and unbuckled his own gun belt, "Better do like he says. I should of stopped Tip before he drawed his gun. But I figured that feller knowed he was just showin' off and wouldn't actually shoot him."

"I didn't know that and you didn't either," Cole Decker said. "I think he meant to kill me, and I don't think any of you would have cared if he had. I want to see some gun belts hit the floor. I won't say it again."

The girl bit her lips as she unbuckled her gun belt and flung it to the floor. The others obeyed more calmly, while watching Decker with hard eyes, already seeing themselves riddling him with hot lead when they were holding the guns.

When all the gun belts were on the floor, Mack glared at Decker and asked, "Do you know who we are?"

"No."

"I'm Mack Adams. Them boys are my brothers and she's our sister."

The girl's dark hair barely reached to the collar of her short jacket. The hatred in her dark eyes leaped at Decker. "You're dead, mister."

"You already said that," Decker said. "I want all of you to take off your coats so I can see what you've got under them." After they had obeyed, he added, "Now pull up your shirts."

"Don't push your luck!" the girl said.

"I can see what you've got under yours," Decker told her.

The one with the twisted face snickered. "She sure sticks out in all the right places, even if she is my sister."

"Shut up, Jinx!" the girl yelled.

Jinx rubbed the grin off his face and studied Decker thoughtfully. Then he looked at the dead boy and said, "I got me a idea. I know y'all plan to hunt that feller down and kill him. Why not let him take Tip over to that old sheriff's office at Rio Blanco and collect the thousand dollar reward on him, so he'll have some money in his pocket when we kill him."

"You're crazy!" the girl said.

The two silent Adams brothers looked sharply at the dead boy. Mack thoughtfully stroked his beard and said, "Reckon there ain't no use lettin' good money go to waste. Pickin's has been slim lately. That last feller we robbed only had a few dollars on him, and his horse wasn't even worth stealin'."

Decker also looked thoughtfully at the dead boy. "I'm on my way to Rio Blanco."

Mack Adams looked at him with hatred in his black eyes and said grudgingly, "We'll put Tip on his horse and leave it tied out front, then wait in the saloon till you're gone."

"I don't believe this," the girl said as she led the way out of the restaurant.

Jinx was right behind her, grinning at the natural wobble of her backside. "You done outgrowed them tight farm pants, Kate."

Kate turned and slapped the grin off his face. "Shut up, Jinx. You should be helpin' Crane carry Tip outside, instead of walkin' out and leavin' it for Tug to do. He's almost twice your age."

"Not hardly. He's only thirty-nine, a year younger than Mack. I'm twenty-three, more'n two years older than Tip was. Anyway, it was my idea. Somebody else should tote him outside and put him on his horse."

"You've always got some excuse not to do nothin' but drive me crazy!"

Tug and Crane carried Tip outside. They had been careful to leave his gun lying on the floor where he had dropped it when he fell. Mack followed them with Tip's hat. At the door he turned his hard black eyes toward Decker.

"We'll be seein' you."

"It better not be too soon. It will probably take a week or more to get the money."

"It better not take no week or more," Mack Adams said. "You better sell him to that old sheriff for a little less and start ridin'."

"I'll see what I can do."

Decker watched the door until it closed behind Mack Adams. Then he holstered his gun and began gathering up the guns and gun belts that belonged to the Adams gang, while Hoola watched with interest.

"You got a sack that will hold all this hardware?" he asked.

She found a sack in the kitchen and handed it across the counter to him. "Looks like you're in the bounty huntin' business again."

"Not again," he said as he put the guns and cartridge belts in the flour sack. "This is the first time."

"I seem to recall that you ended up with some bounty money that Snot Wagner stole from a poor old widow woman."

"I didn't figure Snot would need it where he was going. And I was afraid if I tried to return the money to Ma Webb, she'd shoot me."

"You comin' back?" Hoola asked.

"You think you'll still be here?"

"I sort of doubt it. If I don't get away from Red Frisby, he's gonna have a heart attack some night tryin' to prove he's man enough for me. He's started spendin' his days restin' and tryin' to recover in the room behind the kitchen. He's back there now, about half dead."

Decker looked at her with tortured eyes. "You're a bad girl." If he meant it as a joke, it didn't sound like one.

"Ain't that the kind of girl all men really want?" she asked.

"I don't know about all men. I want a nice, pretty girl that I can trust."

"Like Betty Lovett? I heard she accidentally shot Sam Hayton, then decided to stay at that ranch and stage station and help Cindy Hayton run the place. Just those two pretty girls there now and nobody to protect them from those wild young cowboys and all kinds of men spendin' the night there."

Decker looked closely at the tall, dark-haired beauty. "It sounds to me like you're jealous."

"I am. I'd go back there if I wasn't afraid Cindy Hayton would run me off with a shotgun."

"She probably would. She made sure you didn't stay long that rainy night a while back." He hefted the heavy sack. "Tell the Adams gang I'll leave their guns somewhere in the desert west of town.

Maybe that will slow them down a little."

The four Adams men and their shapely younger sister cussed savagely and bitterly when Hoola told them what Decker had said.

"I figured he'd leave them here," Mack Adams said.

"You ain't dealin' with a fool," Hoola said.

"We're the fools!" Kate cried. "We ain't even got enough money to buy more guns with! We better borrow a gun from somebody and stick up that general store. They've got some."

"We ain't stickin' up that general store," Mack Adams said. "The man who runs it is a old bull. He keeps a double-barreled shotgun on the counter when we're in town. Maybe we can find our guns. I figure that feller throwed them over in the brush without leavin' the road, so there wouldn't be no tracks to lead us to them."

It turned out that Mack Adams was half right, as he said later. They soon found a pistol with no cartridges in it. Almost an hour later they found a cartridge belt and holster, but there were no cartridges in the belt loops.

"Son of a bitch!" Mack Adams said hoarsely. "I'll bet he kept all our shells! And there ain't no tellin' how long it will take us to find our guns."

"What good will they do us anyway, if they're all empty?" Kate asked disgustedly. "We ain't even got enough money between us to buy a box of shells! It looks like some of us will have to get a job before we starve."

Jinx grinned. "You could prob'ly get a job at that restaurant, Kate. That tall girl said she was gonna quit."

"She also said he only hired her so he could sleep with her! But so far he ain't paid her nothin' 'cause he ain't got no money. Why don't you just shut up, before I slap that silly grin off your face!"

CHAPTER 2

A tall bearded man in a wide-brimmed hat stood looking out over the saloon's batwing doors at the empty street. He had very cold pale blue eyes under dark brows. He had won the saloon in a poker game, but sometimes he suspected that the previous owner had let him win so he wouldn't have to abandon the place. It was beginning to look like that was what Rufus Brown would have to do.

Rufus Brown hadn't always been his name, but that was the name he had decided to use when he had ridden into the almost deserted town of Adobe Wells six months ago.

The plank bar ran along one wall of the big dim room. A big pot-bellied, bucktoothed man stood behind the bar watching Brown with large protruding eyes. He said in a nasal drawl, "I hate to keep bringin' it up, Rufe, but you ain't paid me nothin' since I went to work here three months ago."

Rufus Brown scowled. "Christ, Baldy, if I charged you for all the booze you drink and all the free lunch you eat, you'd owe me money."

"Ain't hardly been no customers lately, before them outlaws showed up," Baldy Skall said. "I didn't figger there was no use lettin' all them sandwiches go to waste."

"They're all gone before anybody else gets a chance to eat any. Ain't none left now. I think I'll go to the restaurant and see what Hoola's got cooked."

"She shore is a looker. But I think I'd ruther have that outlaw girl. Did you see how she filled out them tight pants. Even her brother, the one she called Jinx and didn't seem to like, couldn't keep his eyes off her backside."

Rufus Brown left the saloon without answering and headed for the small restaurant where Hoola worked. He found her standing behind the counter as usual. She offered no greeting, but watched him with her bold dark eyes as he stepped up to the counter and took a stool. He pushed his hat back and said, "You got anything good to eat?"

"Just me. Them outlaws ate up everything I had cooked and I'm too lazy to cook anything till supper. But I've got a pot of hot coffee."

"I guess I'll have to settle for that." She brought him a cup and he thoughtfully took a few sips of the strong black liquid, then set the cup down and said, "What all do you know about that feller who shot Tip Adams?"

Hoola's dark eyes went blank. "Not much."

Rufus Brown gave her a closer look and noticed that she was dark enough to be a Mexican or an Indian, but didn't look much like either. Not that it mattered. With a face and figure like hers, the color of her skin seemed unimportant.

He remembered that he needed money and said, "You catch his name?"

"Seems like he said it was John Smith."

"Think that's his real name?"

She shrugged. "When a man tells me his name is Smith or Brown, I figure he don't want me to know his real name."

Rufus Brown smiled. "How did you get a name like Hoola?"

"My pa said I used to say that all the time when I was tryin' to learn how to talk. So he started callin' me that."

"What's your real name?"

She met his glance and said, "Jane Smith."

"You any kin to John Smith?"

"No. But I wouldn't have to change my name if I married him."

"Do you want to marry him?"

"I might not turn him down if he asked me to. He's a very interestin' man for someone who doesn't have much to say. And he likes to travel around the country. That's what I like to do. I figure I'll be gone by the end of the week."

He watched her closely as he said, "To look for John Smith?"

She returned his glance and her eyes were disillusioned and almost sad. "I usually just start ridin' and end up with whoever's lookin' for me."

"I'll keep that in mind." He took another sip of coffee and then asked, "You think the Adams gang will catch up with John Smith?"

"They better hope not."

Sheriff Felix Peabody was a small dried-up old man who often wondered why they didn't elect a sheriff who knew what he was doing and wasn't afraid to do it. His hat looked too big on his small head. His gray mustache looked too big for his face and made him look ridiculous. But the people of Rio Blanco and the surrounding county seemed to want a sheriff who didn't take himself too seriously or cause them too much trouble.

He stood at the door of his office looking from Cole Decker to the dead man tied across the buckskin's saddle.

"Bounty hunter, huh? Well, it's good money, but dangerous work. I want you gone soon as I can get the money back, so them other Adamses won't come here lookin' for you and start slingin' lead in every direction. They might hit me."

"The sooner I get the money, the sooner I'll be gone," Cole Decker said.

He was eating a late breakfast in the small restaurant across the street the next morning when the slightly reduced Adams gang rode boldly into town and drew rein in front of the sheriff's office. Felix Peabody came to the door and listened to their complaints.

Decker heard him say, "Only one gun and no shells for it, huh? I'm tempted to collect some bounties my own self."

The angry girl yelled, "Floyd Hamby and his men will kill you if you do!"

"That's what I'm afraid of," the sheriff said. "Seems like I heard he was related to y'all somehow. Y'all best ride on out there and stay with him till Cole Decker leaves town."

"So that's his name," Kate Adams said as she and her brothers rode on out of town heading west. "I knowed it wasn't John Smith, like he told that saloonkeeper."

Jinx snickered. "That saloonkeeper's name prob'ly ain't Rufus Brown, neither."

"I never said it was. But he ain't no bounty hunter."

"I wouldn't bet no money on that," Mack Adams said, looking uneasily back over his shoulder.

Jinx snickered again. "Ain't none of us got no money. That's why I said we should let Decker collect the bounty on Tip, so he'd have some money when we kill him."

"Don't remind me," Kate said. "The way our luck's been goin', he may collect the bounty on some more of us, if we ain't careful."

They pushed their tired horses along the stage road as though a posse were right behind them, not slowing down much until they saw the big adobe house half hidden in a grove of old cottonwood trees. There were other buildings beyond the house, but the riders paid no attention to them. They halted in a cloud of dust in front of the main house, and Floyd Hamby appeared at the door with a gun in his hand, his mean bloodshot eyes glaring at them and past them.

"Somebody chasin' y'all?" he asked.

Mack Adams rubbed his chin and studied the burly man uneasily. "Not as far as I know."

Floyd Hamby looked at the sweaty horses and his face turned red with rage behind the short, dirty beard. "Then why in hell are y'all tryin' to ride them horses to death? Them horses is mine till I get paid for them. I made that clear when I let y'all take them. I said it two or three times. Where's that fine buckskin I loaned Tip?"

"Tip's dead, Floyd," Mack Adams said. "A stranger killed him in Adobe Wells yesterday mornin'."

"I'm surprised somebody didn't kill him a long time ago. Where's that buckskin I loaned him?"

"That feller who killed him brought his body to Rio Blanco on him, Floyd. He's gonna wait in Rio till the sheriff gets the reward money back. Then he'll prob'ly start ridin' and try to get away with all that reward money. But we'll be right behind him. These horses will be rested up by then and we will too."

Floyd Hamby's bearded face got even redder. "Them's my horses. I ain't heard you say nothin' about payin' me for them."

"We'll have plenty of money to pay you with after we kill that feller and get that bounty money, Floyd," Mack Adams said, watching Hamby with worried eyes.

"You said you'd come back and pay me for the horses in a few months," Hamby growled. "That was a year ago. Now you're back and talkin' about payin' me when you kill some stranger and get the bounty money he's gonna collect for killin' Tip. He'll prob'ly kill some more of you."

"That's just what I told them," Kate Adams said.

Floyd Hamby looked at her with interest.

CHAPTER 3

Luck was with Cole Decker the night he rode away from Rio Blanco on his dark chestnut with the buckskin on a lead rope. A few drops of rain were already falling and the rain started coming down hard while the Adams gang chased him across the desert. The five swearing outlaws lost sight of him in the darkness and the pouring rain, and following his trail was out of the question. So they separated and all five of them got lost looking for him. By the time the hidden sun was trying to rise behind the overcast, the Adamses were looking for one another. They had lost all hope of finding Cole Decker anytime soon.

By the time they all got back together, Kate was so mad she slapped Jinx and the others had to pull them apart. Jinx was getting the worst of it and complained that Kate didn't fight fair.

The outlaws separated again and rode like hell in four different directions, north, south, east, and west.

Mack and Kate rode west, Tug rode north, Jinx rode south after flipping a coin with Crane, who rode east back the way they had come and none of them wanted to go, believing a posse was far more likely to be found in that direction than the man they were looking for.

It was a little past noon when Crane Adams rode into Adobe Wells, the little town where Tip Adams had got himself killed. The rain had stopped for a while but the overcast sky promised more soon. The muddy street was deserted except for two horses tied in front of the restaurant. Crane Adams knuckled his eyes and gazed in disbelief at the dark chestnut and the buckskin.

In the restaurant, Cole Decker sat on a stool finishing a leisurely meal and quietly studying the small, dried-up old man who stood behind the counter looking wistfully out the window. The small old man looked half dead.

"Did Hoola quit?" Decker finally asked.

The small old man behind the counter sighed and nodded. His dry lips moved but no words came out.

"She leave town?"

"Uh-huh."

"Say where she was headed?"

"Said something about goin' back to Hayton's and tryin' to talk Cindy Hayton into lettin' her stay there a while. A feller who came by there said Cindy fired that Mexican cook."

Cole Decker laid some money on the counter, rose and strolled outside. A rider was coming along the street on a tired horse. It was Crane Adams. He stared at Cole Decker with wide eyes and suddenly went for his gun. It was half out of the holster when Decker's bullet knocked him off his horse. He hit the muddy street on his back, tried to rise and then collapsed with a loud grunt.

CHAPTER 4

Decker got the dead man's gun and looked along the empty street in both directions. He saw no more outlaws approaching and the townspeople were staying inside the frame and adobe buildings. Then the saloon's batwing doors creaked and the tall bearded man stepped outside smoking a cigar and turned crafty eyes toward Decker. Decker shoved Crane Adams's gun in his waistband and tied the dead outlaw's horse beside his dark chestnut, then strolled down the street toward the saloonkeeper.

"He a friend of yours?" Decker asked.

The saloonkeeper shook his head. "Him and his brothers and that girl have stopped here a few times. I doubt if they've got any friends."

"They're all worth a thousand dollars apiece except Mack, who's worth fifteen hundred," Decker said. "I'll sell that one to you for eight hundred."

"What makes you think I've got that kind of money?" the saloonkeeper asked.

"Just a hunch. I figure the sheriff is already on his way here, because he thinks I went west and they all followed me. My guess is he headed in what he thought was the safest direction."

The saloonkeeper laughed. "You're probably right about that."

"You could make two hundred dollars real easy," Decker said.

The saloonkeeper thoughtfully smoked his cigar and studied the body of the dead outlaw. Then he grinned and said, "It's a deal. Come inside and I'll pay you."

Decker glanced along the street again and then followed the bearded man into the saloon. He looked silently at the big fat man who stood behind the bar. Everything about Baldy Skall seemed too big—his bald head, his bold protruding eyes, his beak of a nose, his buckteeth, and his potbellied body. Decker had been in the saloon before and the saloonkeeper had introduced himself as Rufus Brown and had tilted his head at Baldy Skall and mentioned his name.

"Drink?" Rufus Brown asked now.

"No thanks. I'm sort of in a hurry."

The saloonkeeper laughed. "I figured you were." Glancing about the empty room, he took out a wallet and frowned when he saw Baldy Skall staring hungrily at it. He turned his back on the big man, counted out some money and handed it to Decker.

Having watched the saloonkeeper count the money, Decker said, "This is a thousand."

The saloonkeeper nodded, studying him with friendly eyes. "I guess you don't remember me?"

Decker studied the saloonkeeper's handsome bearded face and shook his head. "Just when I was in here the other day."

"I recognized you then, but after you said your name was John Smith, almost like you were getting even with me for saying mine was Rufus Brown, I decided that you probably didn't want to be recognized. A lot of people don't, and it's not always because they're wanted by the law."

He made a brief gesture. "The first time I saw you was in Louisiana, right after the war. I believe you were on your way home from Georgia or someplace. I wasn't going nowhere fast. Two fellers had just shot me off my horse to rob me and were about to finish me when you came along. The wind was making a lot of noise in the trees and they never even noticed you until you stopped your horse and said, 'War's over.' Then they turned their guns to shoot you, but it was you who did the shooting. You got me to a doctor and wouldn't take a penny for it, even though I knew you were broke. The South had lost the war and almost everything else. I don't forget favors like that, but I never figured I'd get a chance to do you one."

Decker studied the man's face again. "You didn't have a beard then, just a mustache. And you looked like a fancy gambler. That's probably why they decided to rob you. They figured you had money."

"I was also more than ten years younger," Rufus Brown said.

"We both were," Decker said. "I'm Cole Decker."

"I've heard the name, but didn't know it belonged to you. You never mentioned your name or said anything about yourself when you saved my bacon back in '65. Chances are you've heard some unsavory things said about me, but I've never done anything I'm ashamed of."

Decker nodded. "I better be going. I'll leave that outlaw's horse where it is. It can be used to carry him to the county seat." He glanced at the money in his hand. "Thanks for the favor."

"It's nothing compared to what you did for me."

"It could cause you trouble with the Adams gang."

"I'm not worried. After I recovered from getting bushwhacked by those boys in Louisiana, I learned how to handle a gun and I've had to use one several times. I'm almost as well known as you are."

Cole Decker glanced about the empty saloon. "How did you end up running a saloon in a nearly deserted town like this?"

"I won it from the previous owner in a poker game and now I'm stuck with it. I'll probably have to abandon it if I don't find a buyer soon."

More than a week after Cole Decker left, the four surviving members of the Adams gang rode into Adobe Wells and tramped into the saloon. Rufus Brown stood at the bar talking to his bartender, turning his watchful dark eyes as the four angry people came in.

"You son of a bitch!" Kate Adams said.

Mack Adams made a tired gesture with one hand while knocking dust from his clothes with the other. "I'll do the talkin', Kate. Rufus, I thought you was our friend. What's the idea of helpin' that feller you knowed we was lookin' for?"

"He saved my life once," Rufus Brown said. "I tried to do him and y'all too a favor."

"I don't foller you. How could you do both him and us a favor?"

"There were six of you the last time you came here. Now there's only four. The next time you run into Cole Decker, there will be even fewer of you left."

"The next time we run into him, we'll kill him!" Kate Adams said.

Rufus Brown glanced at her. His eyes strayed almost imperceptibly to her curves. "It was mainly because of you that I helped Decker, Kate. I hated to think what might happen if he hung around long enough to collect the bounty on Crane and you caught up with him. He'd hate to kill a pretty girl, but not enough to let you kill him."

Jinx's hairy mouth twisted in a dirty grin. "I suspicioned you had the hots for her, Rufus."

"Shut up, Jinx!" Kate cried. "Wipe that silly grin off your face!"

"I never said I blamed him," Jinx said. "If you wasn't my sister—"

Yelling her rage, Kate swung her fist at Jinx's bearded face and knocked him staggering into Tug, who shoved him away and said, "Damn, Jinx. Why don't you leave her alone?"

"Why don't she leave me alone?" Jinx retorted. "The next time she hits me—"

"Both of you cut it out," Mack Adams said hoarsely, a baffled look on his dark face. "We didn't come here for that."

Then he said to the saloonkeeper, "If what you say is true, Rufus, I reckon I can't blame you for tryin' to git Decker away from here before we caught up with him."

Rufus Brown smiled with relief. "I'm glad to hear you say that, Mack. Maybe I can do you a favor. I know y'all ain't had much luck in the outlaw business in quite a spell, and things ain't likely to improve none now that Crane and Tip are dead. If you had this saloon, you could hole up here until the stages start running again and carrying more money. You being a friend of mine, I'd sell it to you real cheap. I'm hankering to move on anyway. I never was cut out to be a saloonkeeper."

Mack Adams looked at him with shocked eyes. "I can't believe you'd try to unload this dump on me, Rufus. It's gettin' so a man can't even trust his friends these days. I doubt if you're makin' enough money here to pay your bartender."

"He ain't makin' enough to pay me," Baldy Skall said. His marble eyes rolled all over Kate's curves before shifting back to Mack. "And I'm tired of wonderin' when some law dog or bounty hunter will turn up and remember seein' my face on two or three dozen wanted posters. Fact is, I wouldn't mind joinin' up with y'all, Mack."

"It looks like we can use you," Mack Adams said. "But right now all we've got planned is huntin' Cole Decker down and killin' him and dividin' that bounty money he collected on Crane and Tip. If you ride with us, you'll have to earn your share, and that means helpin' us get Decker."

"That won't bother me none," Baldy Skall said. "It's because of that bastard that I need to get outta here. Them two killin's he done in this town will have bounty hunters driftin' this way like buzzards at the smell of dead meat."

"I don't think that's the only reason you want to ride with us,"

Jinx Adams said.

"Shut your dirty mouth, Jinx," Kate Adams said. "Everybody don't think like you."

"You'll see," Jinx said.

Rufus Brown frowned at Baldy Skall. "If you quit, I'll have to close this place, Baldy."

Baldy Skall snorted as he took off his dirty white apron and flung it contemptuously aside. "You been talkin' about closin' it and takin' up bounty huntin' anyway. All I can say is, you better not ever come after me. I won't try to outdraw you. I'll hide behind a rock and fill you full of buckshot. This here's my scattergun under the bar and I'm takin' it with me."

Rufus Brown looked uneasily at the sawed-off, double-barreled shotgun as Baldy Skall broke the gun open to check the loads. "I thought we were friends, Baldy."

Baldy Skall took a battered hat and a dirty wool coat down from a peg as he came out from behind the bar. "You ain't got no friends, Rufus, 'cause nobody can't trust you. I heard you tell Decker the Adams gang didn't have no friends. But you sure'n hell ain't got none. Decker's a fool if he thinks you're his friend just because you decided to do him a favor. If I know you, you'll close this place down soon as we leave and foller along like a scavenger, hopin' to get your hands on Decker's money after we kill him, and maybe collect some fresh bounties besides. But like I said, you better not come after me, 'less you want your carcass filled full of buckshot."

"You ain't thinking straight, as usual," Rufus Brown said. "I wasn't planning on collecting any bounties on men who're still alive. But what if some more of you boys get killed? It's possible, going after a man like Cole Decker. If it happens, you need somebody along to collect the reward money on them. Somebody who's not wanted by the law. No use letting good money go to waste, or leave the bodies for the first bounty hunter who comes along."

"Which would be you," Baldy Skall said.

"Not if I'm working with you fellers. All I want is a share of the bounty money for helping y'all get it."

"Makes sense to me," Kate Adams said. "If something was to happen to Jinx—"

Both Jinx and Rufus Brown laughed, but nobody else did. Kate seemed completely serious. Baldy Skall watched her with thinly disguised lust and Rufus Brown with open suspicion. Mack and Tug

Adams looked like they were going to their own funeral.

There was a look of doom in Mack's dark eyes even as he said, "A man like Rufus, who ain't wanted by the law or a known outlaw, can be useful to us in a lot of different ways, especially if it don't get out that he's ridin' with us. He can ride into strange towns and size things up without causin' any suspicion, and he can pick up supplies in places where we wouldn't dare show our faces."

"I never thought about that," Baldy Skall said. "I just hope he don't sell us out."

Mack Adams turned to Brown. "Rufus, I want you to hang back after we leave, so nobody will know you're ridin' with us now. Make up some story to tell the townsfolks. You can say you've decided to close the saloon and move on now that Baldy has quit on you and joined up with us. We'll wait for you outside of town a piece."

Chapter 5

After scouring the country to the east of Adobe Wells for a week and finding no sign of Cole Decker, the Adams gang with its two new members halted in the drying mud off to the left of an eroded butte and stared at the empty desert ahead. They didn't know how empty it really was, because most of the Apaches and bounty hunters in New Mexico could have hidden in the brush-lined arroyos or behind the scattered rock formations. The sun blazed brightly out of a deep blue sky, but the wind breathed an icy chill at them from the snow-capped mountains.

Mack Adams fished the stub of a cigar from a coat pocket, stuck it between his square teeth, and searched through other pockets for a sulphur match. He glanced at the hostile mountains with sour distaste and said, "He ain't fool enough to go up there, and we can't find no tracks headin' east or south. He musta doubled back on us again durin' the rain. He was likely off to one side headin' back west while we was on our way to Adobe Wells to pick up his trail. He rode east till it started rainin' again and then circled around. That's my guess."

"He's a slick son of a gun all right," Baldy Skall whined. "I'd sure like to get my hands on him. Trouble is, men like him don't hardly ever fight with their fists, 'cept in them dime novels. Real cowboys and gunfighters don't want no part of fistfightin'. But I reckon they won't have no choice when the law takes their guns away, like it's already doin' in some places. They sure'n hell ain't gonna stop fightin' completely."

"Fistfightin' sure don't settle nothin'," Kate said. "I already found that out. My hand's still sore from the last time I hit Jinx, and he's meaner'n ever. He was supposed to ride east instead of Crane. But he got Crane to flip a coin and Crane lost and got hisself killed, and I'm still havin' to put up with Jinx."

"That ain't no way to talk, Kate," Mack Adams said. "Jinx is still your brother."

"He's a jinx," Kate said. "That's how he got that nickname. And sooner or later he'll get us all killed."

"If he don't, I reckon somebody else will," Baldy Skall said, turning his marble-like eyes toward Rufus Brown.

The others also looked at the former saloonkeeper, who sat his horse off to one side, lighting a cigar. He looked at Baldy Skall with hard eyes, but said nothing.

Mack Adams cleared his throat and looked back the way they had come. "It looks like we'll have to split up again, or we'll never find Decker. Rufus, I want you to ride through Rio Blanco and find out if he rode back that way. Me and Kate will swing by that little minin' camp at the foot of the mountains. Tug, you and Jinx and Baldy make a swing to the south of Rio Blanco and ask anybody you see if they've seen a man ridin' a fine lookin' dark chestnut. He might get rid of the buckskin, but he seems attached to that dark chestnut and I don't blame him.

"We'll all meet at Floyd Hamby's place soon as we all get there. You'll likely arrive first, Rufus. Just hang around there till the rest of us arrive."

"Wouldn't it be better if I rode with you and Kate, Mack?" Baldy Skall asked. "It shore would be a pity if her purty black hair ended up decoratin' some Apache's lance."

Jinx laughed. "I knew he'd want to stay with Kate. Ain't y'all noticed how his eyes crawl all over her?"

"It's partly because of you that I want to go with Mack and Kate, Jinx," Baldy Skall said. "I don't think I can put up with much more of yore mouth."

"I don't see how anyone can put up with his mouth!" Kate said. "If we wasn't my brother, I would have killed him before now!"

"Jinx is about the most aggravatin' human I ever saw in my life," Mack Adams said. "Tug is about the only one who can put up with him, now that Crane is dead. Crane just ignored him. I reckon you better ride with us, Baldy. We don't want no trouble among our-selves."

Tug Adams rarely spoke. When he did it was in a blunt, sarcastic way. Now he pointed a stubby finger at Rufus Brown and then at Baldy Skall. "It ain't Jinx I'm worried about. It's them two. I say run them both off now, or we'll regret it later."

"What's got into you, Tug?" Mack asked in surprise. "We've knowed Rufus quite a while, and I think we can trust Baldy. He's in the same boat as us."

"Baldy would strangle his own mother for a two-bit piece," Tug said savagely. "I figure Jinx is right about him bein' after Kate. Ain't you seen the way he looks at her?"

There was a half smile on Mack's rough, bearded face. "Kate's a mighty good lookin' girl. I wouldn't trust a man who didn't look at her. You don't have to worry about her while I'm with her."

Tug Adams shrugged. "It's your funeral. But take my advice and keep a eye on Baldy. Don't leave him alone with her."

"I don't intend to. What's your gripe against Rufus?"

Tug's bushy black brows knitted in a puzzled frown. "I can't quite put my finger on it. He smiles too much, for one thing."

Mack Adams laughed. "Just because you don't never smile, Tug, that don't mean people who do can't be trusted."

Tug Adams shrugged again. "I hope you're right. Come on, Jinx. And wipe that stupid grin off your face. There ain't a damn thing to grin about."

Tug and Jinx cantered off through the rocks and brush. Tug rode in the lead looking straight ahead. Jinx looked back with his sly grin.

Rufus Brown smiled and touched his hat before riding off toward the stage road which would lead him back through Adobe Wells and on west toward Rio Blanco.

"We better get started too," Mack Adams said. He and Kate took the lead, riding side by side. Baldy Skall brought up the rear, his shotgun gripped in his right hand, his big protruding eyes fixed on Kate's shapely backside.

CHAPTER 6

Sheriff Felix Peabody entered the restaurant and stopped in his tracks when he saw Cole Decker sitting on a stool at the counter, eating a bowl of soup and crackers. The small old sheriff's face grew red above the gray mustache. He took a stool off to one side of the tall man and stared at him in bug-eyed disbelief.

Decker appeared to be wearing the same clothes he usually wore—black hat and coat and brown pants that weren't much darker than his tan shirt. But those clothes looked like they had just come out of the Chinese laundry down the street. The coat was pushed back away from his gun.

"How long you been back?" the sheriff asked in a tone of outrage.

Decker barely glanced at him. "Couple of days."

The sheriff shook his head. "I don't believe this, Decker."

"What?"

"That you'd have the gall to come back to my town, after all the trouble you caused me. They don't pay me to spend all my time collectin' bounties for you and seein' that the bodies get buried."

"There'll be more," Decker said.

"More what?"

"More bodies."

The sheriff's jaw dropped. Just then Slim Short, wearing a dirty white apron, came from the kitchen and set a cup of smoking coffee in front of him. Slim had heard the small old sheriff talking and knew he would want a cup of coffee, though he rarely passed up an opportunity to complain about how bad it was. Now the sheriff looked skeptically at the strong black liquid and said, "My stomach ain't up to that black as sin coffee no more, Slim. Not without something to sweeten it. Better bring me one o' your fried apple pies."

"Bring me one too, and some more coffee," Decker said.

"I reckon you can afford it," the sheriff said grudgingly. "I guess you know he charges for refills. Nickel a cup. That's how he makes most of his money."

"No problem."

Being perhaps the most underpaid sheriff in the West, it was a problem for Felix Peabody. He ground his rotting teeth so hard one of them began to throb painfully. And there was no dentist in Rio Blanco. Not even a doctor worthy of the name, though an old cow doctor named Leo Meece had been passing himself off as the town doc ever since anyone could remember, or at least as long as the town had existed. Of course, there were always those who claimed to remember things that had happened in almost every frontier town before the town had even existed. That was what happened when men started believing their own lies and expected everyone else to believe them, no matter how many contradictory versions they invented.

Slim Short came back with two thin turnovers on a tray and a coffeepot from which he refilled Decker's cup. He left the tray on the countertop and took the coffeepot back to the kitchen.

The sheriff and the gunfighter each took a fried apple pie. The sheriff bit into his and cried out at the stab of pain in his bad tooth.

Decker gave him a wondering look. "What's wrong?"

The sheriff went on eating the hard pie despite the pain. "Got a bad tooth. They're all tryin' to rot on me. I told myself if I left them alone, maybe they'd leave me alone. But it didn't work out that way. I'll prob'ly have to get them all pulled out and get me a set of them store teeth. I ain't much lookin' forward to it.

"Reminds me of a old feller from someplace back East who stayed at the hotel for three or four years. His name was Earl Dunn. Mighty polite. Always called me Mr. Peabody. Case you don't recollect, that's my name. Earl had a little money saved up, I reckon, 'cause he never worked. Spent most of his time sittin' around the hotel readin' old newspapers and smilin' polite at everybody he saw. In the summer you'd find him sittin' out on the hotel porch for hours at a time readin' one of his old newspapers and smilin' and noddin' to people who passed by on the street. But in the winter he'd sit in the lobby near the stove where it was warm.

"One night I ate supper in the dinin' room and saw old Earl sittin' in the corner eatin' a bowl of soup. Did I mention that he had store teeth? Them teeth didn't fit too good and they fell out in his soup. He looked around to see if anybody was watchin' and then fished them teeth out of the soup and stuck them back in his mouth and went on eatin' that soup.

"Ever since then, when I see somebody eatin' soup, I wonder if there's a set of store teeth in it."

Cole Decker finished eating his fried apple pie and sat sipping his coffee in silence.

The sheriff's voice droned on. "One night Earl rented him a livery horse and rode out to a dance at the Box C Ranch. That was back around 1870, I guess, a while before the Box C owner, Hunk Cossitt, was killed by Floyd Hamby, the Circle H owner. They had a misunderstandin' over Floyd's wife Maud. Maud ain't no ravin' beauty, but in this country anything in a skirt looks good. Her and Floyd went to the dance that night and she danced a couple of times with Hunk Cossitt and maybe flirted a little, while Floyd watched with his bloodshot eyes. He took Maud home early, before the rain got started.

"Not long after that, Hunk rode over to the Circle H one day at a time when Floyd should of been gone with his hands, only he wasn't. The Circle H ranch house is the first stage stop west of here and Floyd spent a lot of time at home. He was at home that day and he stepped out on the porch with a double barrel shotgun and emptied both barrels into Hunk Cossitt before he could get down off his horse. Floyd claimed Hunk was grinnin' and callin' Maud's name. Nothin' was done about the killin'. Floyd was just protectin' his home.

"Gettin' back to the dance a few weeks earlier, Earl Dunn never went out there to dance. He just liked to sit in a chair against the wall and watch and grin with his store teeth. He was mighty proud of them teeth, even though they was loose and fell out every now and then, especially when he was eatin' or laughin' about something somebody said.

"It started rainin' about midnight and rained the rest of the night. Most of the people at the dance was plannin' to spend the night anyway. The rain stopped about daylight and Earl got his horse and headed back to town. When he got to the Rio Blanco it was out of its banks, which musta come as quite a shock, 'cause it's nearly dry most

of the time. Like most greenhorns, Earl didn't know how dangerous
a flooded stream can be, so he decided to cross, holdin' onto the livery nag's tail, like he'd heard about people doin', and grinnin' with
his store teeth. Earl was always grinnin'. He didn't know no better.
He nearly drowned a couple of times, but he held onto the horse's
tail and finally made it across. Then he discovered he'd lost his store
teeth somewhere in all that water.

"After that he mostly stayed in his room, when he wasn't down
at the river lookin' for his teeth. He thought they mighta washed up
on the bank and he'd spend whole days walkin' down one side and
comin' back up the other. A dep'ty I had then claimed he once found
Earl searchin' way up above where he lost his teeth and told him it
wasn't likely they'd wash upstream.

"Anyway, Earl never found his teeth. After about a month of
lookin', he packed his bags and went back East. I don't know why he
decided to come out here in the first place. But I often wonder what
I'm doin' here, tryin' to pass myself off as a lawman. Any man in town
can outshoot me and any kid over about ten could beat the stuffin'
out of me."

Decker was still sitting there a couple of stools from the small old
sheriff and listening to the drone of his voice with about as much interest as he would have listened to the buzzing of a fly. His thoughts
had drifted away and he was looking out the window at people passing by, some on foot, some on horses, some on wagons. A lot of people
had come to Rio Blanco because of the Apache scare. If somebody saw
unshod pony tracks, the word soon spread and everybody headed for
town, mainly to be part of the crowd they knew they would find there
and talk about the Indian problem. Many whites thought all the Indians should be killed. Putting them on unfenced reservations did no
good. Most of the sympathy for the Indians was back East where no
one had to worry about getting scalped.

The sheriff muttered something about his teeth and then asked,
"What was that you said about bodies? I hope you ain't plannin' to
bring in no more dead outlaws and want me to get the bounty money
for you. I can't spend all my time doin' that."

"How do you spend your time, Sheriff?" Decker asked.

"Right now I'm spendin' most of it tellin' people there prob'ly ain't
no Apaches closer'n a hundred miles. Floyd Hamby is in town stir-
rin' them up. It was one of his hands who saw the tracks of a unshod
horse and thought it might belong to a buck scoutin' the ranch for a

raidin' party. Now Floyd wants all the ranchers and their hands to head for his place and fort up. I think he's about got them persuaded. That will leave all the other ranches around here unprotected. Floyd knows that even if the other ranchers don't. He was always one to think of hisself first and everybody else last."

Cole Decker's cup was empty. He glanced at it and then asked, "Where's the cavalry? Don't they always arrive in the nick of time, with the bugles blowing and the flag waving?"

"Not around here, they don't. The nearest fort's over a hundred miles away. They ain't gonna send a patrol here just because somebody saw the tracks of a unshod horse. It could be a wild horse. These days, Apaches are more likely to have shod horses that they stole.

"I figure they're makin' their way through the country in little bunches, and may steal a few horses but not cause any other trouble, provided nobody gets too close to them. Could the Apaches be the reason you come into town?"

Decker shook his head. "I just wanted to buy a few things."

"I noticed you was all dressed up like you was goin' to a funeral. If you ain't careful, it could be your own."

Chapter 7

Slim Short came from the kitchen and asked, "Ya'll want some more coffee?"

"Not at a nickel a refill," the sheriff said hoarsely. "You must think I'm made outta money."

Even in his baggy old clothes, it was easy to see how Slim Short had got his nickname, and he didn't look very healthy, but his narrow, lined face looked hard as a rock. "Then maybe you'd like to pay now," he said. "You're keepin' my customers scared away."

The sheriff pointed at Cole Decker. "Wasn't nobody here when I got here but him. He's the one who's keepin' your customers scared away. They're afraid he'll shoot them just in case there's a price on their heads."

"I'll buy both me and him another cup of coffee and another fried pie," Decker said, placing a silver dollar on the counter. "You can take everything out of this."

Slim looked at the coin and said, "You got anything smaller? I'm outta change."

"Keep it."

"No more pie for me," the sheriff said. "My bad tooth's already killin' me."

When Slim brought Decker's pie and refilled both Decker's cup and the sheriff's from the coffeepot, the sheriff looked at Decker and said, "Obliged. But a bribe this size won't buy you nothin'. I just re-

membered another problem you caused me. Floyd Hamby has been
snortin' and pawin' the ground about you stealin' his horse."

"I never stole his horse."

"He claims that buckskin Tip Adams was ridin' belongs to him."

"I noticed the Circle H brand. But I've been trying not to think
about it."

"Maybe you should have. Why didn't you leave the horse at the
stable instead of takin' it with you when you made tracks that night?"

"I wanted to ride him part of the time to make it easier on my
horse."

"Floyd won't like you usin' one of his horses to get away from the
Adams gang. He was hopin' they'd catch you and use some of that
reward money to pay him for all the horses they've been ridin' like
drunk Comanches ever since they rode their own horses to death.
They always ride like a posse's right behind them, just in case there
is one."

"I heard they use Floyd Hamby's ranch as a hideout part of the
time," Decker said.

"I ain't sayin' they do and I ain't sayin' they don't," the sheriff said
cautiously. "For all I know, they may hang around there part of the
time on account of Maud. I wouldn't call her pretty, but there's something about her. She came through here on a stage in '69, when she
was around twenty but looked like she'd already done a lot of livin'.
Stopped at the hotel a few days and asked Bossy Bittle, the hotel
lady, about a job as a waitress. Bossy said she didn't need anyone,
but she told me later that Maud looked like a saloon girl who was
down on her luck."

He took a sip of coffee, sighed with satisfaction and went on,
"Maud took the next westbound stage and stopped at Floyd Hamby's
place. The next I heard, they were livin' together and claimed to be
married. The hands say her and Floyd fight like cats and dogs."

Slim stood behind the counter looking out the window with worried eyes. "I see Floyd Hamby comin' now," he said and retreated to
the kitchen with the coffeepot.

Cole Decker turned sideways on his stool so he could watch the
door. He was already holding the cup in his left hand so his right
hand would be free to grab his gun if necessary. He went on sipping
his coffee and watched the door with his clear gray eyes.

The man who opened the door and came in was broad and heavy.
His eyes were small and mean and his dark-bearded face looked swol-

len and contorted with a savage rage against anything that got in his way or caused him any trouble.

Sheriff Felix Peabody had turned completely around on his stool and he held his coffee cup carefully in both gnarled hands. His eyes looked old and faded and worried. "'Lo, Floyd," he said in a cautious tone. "I thought you and them others was about ready to ride out to your place."

Floyd Hamby replied in a harsh, scornful voice, "Them fools talked it over and decided to go back to their own places. It'll serve them right if they all git scalped."

"There may not be no trouble," the sheriff said. "Sometimes the Apaches sneak through the country without—"

Floyd Hamby snorted. "The last time they drove off some of my horses. But it seems like they ain't the only horse thieves around here. The old man at the stable told me the feller who stole my buckskin rode back into town a coupla days ago on a dark chestnut and was still leadin' Buck just like he owned him. Said he saw him come in here a little while ago."

"No call to talk that way, Floyd," the sheriff said. "It's just a misunderstandin', that's all."

"Why you tryin' to protect him, Peabody?" Floyd Hamby asked suspiciously.

The sheriff looked surprised. "I ain't tryin' to protect him, Floyd. I'm tryin' to protect you."

Floyd Hamby scowled. "What's that supposed to mean?"

"Christ, Floyd, he's already killed Crane and Tip Adams, and either one of them coulda shot rings around you."

Floyd Hamby snorted. "Who says they coulda?"

"They did. I heard them braggin' in the saloon about courtin' Maud right in front of you and you was afraid to say anything about it. But later you told Mack he better put a stop to it or there was gonna be trouble."

"There was gonna be trouble, too!"

"You wouldn't of tried to get Mack to stop it if you hadn't been afraid of them, Floyd."

"Who says I wouldn't?"

"You threatened to kill Jinx for doin' the same thing. You was talkin' about it in the saloon, your own self."

"I was talkin' to the bartender, a old friend o' mine," Floyd Hamby said in a tone of outrage. "I didn't know there was anybody else in the saloon. But you snuck in and was listenin' with both ears. And you told everybody you saw what I said! I'm tired of you tellin' lies about me."

"I ain't told no lies about you, Floyd," the old sheriff muttered.

"Like hell! I know you've told people I murdered Tony Hill and buried his body somewhere on my ranch. When you say things like that you're askin' to get yourself killed. I've put up with that kinda talk all I'm goin' to. And now I find you settin there swappin' lies with a man who stole my horse."

"That ain't so," the sheriff stammered.

Cole Decker set his cup on the counter and rose to his feet, facing the angry man standing just inside the door. "I thought the horse belonged to Tip Adams, a man who tried to kill me," he said. "I didn't know he belonged to you till the sheriff told me a few minutes ago."

"You knowed he didn't belong to you."

"I doubt if he belongs to you either. Your brand was burned over the Box C brand. Not a very good job, either."

"That don't concern you. I got tired of Hunk Cossitt tryin' to put his brand on my wife, so I shot the bastard and took over his ranch."

Cole Decker smiled a thin, sour smile. "And you're raising hell about me using a horse I thought belonged to a man who tried to kill me. Get out of here and leave me alone, before I kill you."

He said it in such a quiet, indifferent way that Floyd Hamby gave him a wondering look and asked, "What did you say?"

Cole Decker watched the hairy man through frozen gray eyes and said nothing more.

The sheriff was smiling happily. "You better git outta here, Floyd, while you can. There ain't a price on your head, is there?"

"No, there ain't no price on my head," Floyd Hamby said and turned to go. Then he swung back around and said to the sheriff, "How did you find out—who told you I killed Tony Hill?"

"Some of your hands were talkin' about it in the saloons."

A really wild look came into Floyd Hamby's eyes. "Sons of bitches!" he said in a voice choked with anger. Turning, he jerked the door open and slammed it behind him so hard the windows rattled.

Standing at the door a short time later, Cole Decker saw Hamby ride away from the stable on a big bay, leading the buckskin with the badly altered brand.

Cussing and crying in his frustrated rage, Floyd Hamby galloped and cantered most of the way to his ranch house. His men heard him coming and came out of the bunkhouse, expecting trouble because of his hurry. There were five of them, all in their twenties or early thirties. They all wore dirty range clothes and all packed cartridge belts and holstered Colts. Their eyes were worried as Floyd Hamby swung down from his saddle, for his bearded face was red and contorted with an old rage that always seemed ready to explode into violence.

"You sons of bitches!" he roared. "I told y'all to keep your mouths shut when you went to town the other night!"

"It was Shorty," said Carl Leach, the tallest and toughest one of the five. "After we left the Ace High, he wanted to stop at Fat Al's place 'cause Fat threw him out a while back when he went there by hisself. He's been dyin' to get even with Big Al ever since. He didn't cause no trouble when we stopped there the other night, but he told Big Al the same thing that happened to Tony Hill might happen to him if he wasn't careful."

"Shorty, you stupid son of a bitch!" Floyd Hamby said.

The small cowhand called Shorty was backing up with his mouth open and his hands out in a pleading gesture when Floyd Hamby's big pistol boomed and knocked him flat on his back.

Chapter 8

"We'll stop here long enough to blow the horses," Mack Adams said, not bothering to consult Baldy Skall or even glance back at him. "Been pushin' them pretty hard."

They had stopped in the middle of nowhere. A steep wall of mountains rose ahead. The country between them and the mountains was streaked with brush-lined arroyos and rocky ridges where more stunted brush and a little bleached grass grew.

Kate Adams stretched her long arms and turned her body a little to one side as though she wanted Baldy Skall to see her left breast pushing out against her shirt and short jacket. And Baldy Skall, in the grip of savage lust, told himself there was no point in waiting any longer. This might be the best chance he would get.

He raised the shotgun, cocked the right hammer, and shot Mack Adams off his horse. Kate looked in disbelief at her oldest and most dependable brother twitching and dying on the ground, then turned her black head and stared in horror and hatred at Baldy Skall and the shotgun in his hands.

"You killed him!" she cried. "Tug and Jinx were right about you!"

"Shut up and git off that horse!" Baldy snarled.

Instead of obeying, she spurred her horse and galloped away. Cussing, Baldy Skall raised the shotgun, then lowered it and spurred his own horse after her. He wanted her alive. But he knew catching her would not be easy. She had the best horse and she was a better rider, besides weighing less than half as much as Baldy Skall, who tipped the scales at two fifty.

Kate moved away as though shot from a gun and soon disappeared over the next ridge. Spurring and beating his horse with his big fist, Baldy Skall reached that point only a few minutes later and saw her spotted Appaloosa flash over a more distant ridge. She was long gone by the time Baldy got to the top of that ridge. But her trail was fairly easy to follow and he stuck to it until he found the Appaloosa, still saddled, grazing near a rainwater pool near the foot of another rough, steep slope. He saw no sign of Kate.

Getting down carefully with the sawed-off shotgun gripped in his huge right hand, Skall tied his horse to the limb of a dark mesquite tree at the edge of the tall dead grass that surrounded the pool. He started toward the Appaloosa, but the horse lifted its head, snorted, and seemed on the point of bolting. Horses had never liked Baldy Skall. He decided to leave the nervous animal alone, and tramped through the tall grass to the pool. The pool had shrunk in the sun and wind, leaving a rim of drying mud between the water and the grass. And there Baldy Skall found some small boat tracks, moccasin prints, and a little patch of trampled earth where a violent struggle had taken place.

A gleam of white under a low bush drew his attention. Bending down, he saw that it was Kate's ivory-handled revolver. He got the gun and shoved it in his waistband, then gazed in every direction over the tall grass. Rough, rising ground surrounded him on all sides and he could not see far. He found himself staring at a patch of thick brush tall enough to hide a horse and rider. A cottonwood and several mesquite trees rose above the brush. Lowering his gaze, he saw where the grass had been bent down by someone going toward the tall brush. He knew the trail had been made by the Indian wearing moccasins, probably an Apache. He had attacked Kate and with little doubt had made her his capture by knocking her unconscious with a rifle or a club.

Baldy Skall felt certain the Indian was hiding in that thicket and watching him at this very moment, perhaps over the barrel of a rifle. With terror in his wide eyes, Baldy Skall hurried back to his horse and spurred him back the way he had come.

The Appaloosa watched the big man gallop away, then went back to grazing.

After a while, a lone Indian left the dark thicket and slowly approached the Appaloosa with his hand out, talking quietly.

The Indian had a Spencer rifle in his other hand.

CHAPTER 9

After supper in the hotel dining room that night, Cole Decker sat in the warm lobby a while smoking a cigar, telling himself just one wouldn't hurt. He had quit smoking years ago, but every now and then the smell of a good cigar made him long for one. This was the first time he had given in to the old craving. He wondered if it was because he had a good deal of money in his pocket. The main reason he had stopped smoking in leaner times was because he couldn't afford it. He had never known anyone who quit smoking for health reasons. The country and the times were so wild and dangerous, most men considered it a miracle if they lived long enough to die from smoking. Others didn't believe smoking would hurt them. They knew people who had smoked all their lives and never had any health problems. That was proof enough for them.

Decker was not the only one smoking in the hotel lobby that cold, windy night. A small old man named Cox, who had a bad limp, had the stub of a cheap cigar clamped between his yellow teeth. He kept getting up to put more wood in the potbellied stove from the stack in the corner, although Decker had heard the hotel lady complaining to him about using so much wood. Cox lived in the hotel, as did the other two old men who sat in comfortable chairs near the stove. One was fat and nearly bald and wore spectacles. He bore a noticeable resemblance to a picture of Ben Franklin that Decker had once seen. His name was Mr. Diggs.

The third old man was Mr. Slocum. He wore a wide-brimmed cowboy hat and high-heeled cowboy boots but said he was from St. Louis. A little earlier, he had told a story about finding a thick roll of money lying in the street in that city. He said he had not worked a day since finding all that money. He appeared to be around sixty, which made him considerably younger than Mr. Diggs and Mr. Cox.

Decker idly wondered if those three old men had been here in Earl Dunn's time, but he didn't ask. The sheriff had told him all he wanted to know about Earl Dunn.

"Bossy will be in here complainin' about you usin' all that wood, Cox," Mr. Diggs said with a benevolent smile.

"She gets it for nearly nothin' from that Mexican," Cox said as he limped back to his chair. He had the one closest to the stove. "She shouldn't complain anyway, after all the work I do around here just for my room and board. I'm usually the one who lets her know when somebody wants a room. She won't hire a clerk. I get up early every mornin' and build the fires. I peel potatoes, wait on tables, you name it."

Mr. Diggs chuckled. "I ain't heard you askin' for a raise."

Cox rubbed his leathery old face and looked with satisfaction at the red glow of the ancient iron stove. "I don't expect no pay," he said. "It's hard to get enough money out of her for a cigar and a drink every now and then. If it wasn't for Floyd Hamby, I'd move out to that stage station."

"He owns the place!" Mr. Diggs said.

"I know he does," Cox said, still watching the stove and apparently enjoying the crackling sound of the flames devouring the mesquite wood. "I wonder how much he knows about Maud, only that ain't her real name. Tony Hill told me her real name was Milly Rood. He used to know her in Texas, but he said she acted like she'd never seen him before he went to work for Floyd. He said he hadn't told Floyd about knowin' her when she was Milly Rood, back in San Antonio. But maybe Floyd found out and killed him. That's what I'm beginnin' to think."

Decker's cigar was forgotten. He sat gazing past Mr. Diggs and Mr. Slocum at the small, gimpy old man they called Cox. But he wasn't thinking about Cox or the other two old men. He was thinking about Milly Rood.

Decker had been in San Antonio in the early spring of 1869, looking for a job. One evening he had gone to a saloon and sat by himself sipping a glass of beer.

"Want some company?' a quiet voice said.

He looked up to see a slender girl of about twenty, with a rather plain face but beautiful golden-brown hair, already pulling back a chair at his table. She sat down, studied him for a moment with unreadable eyes that were far older than her years, and then said, "I'm Milly Rood. I'm from Kansas and a lot of other places. I usually work as a waitress. This is the first saloon I've ever worked in and I'm only working here because it was the only job I could find. The truth is, I'm hoping some rich man will ask me to marry him or be his mistress."

Decker smiled uncomfortably. "I'm not a rich man."

"You must not be poor, wearing clothes like those."

"Don't let the clothes fool you. I've got a weakness for nice clothes. These won't be nice long, if I can find a job on some ranch. That's what I do most of the year. In the winter I drift."

She shrugged. "People do what they have to or want to, usually some of both. I sure don't plan on doing this for long. I've slept with a few men since I went to work here, but if I don't like their looks I tell them to pick another girl."

Decker tried another smile. It did not feel any more comfortable on his face than the last one. "I guess you look at the clothes first."

Milly Rood frowned. "That's right. And yours fooled me."

Without another word she got up and moved away. When Decker left the saloon she was sitting at a table with a smiling drummer, watching him with her old, unreadable eyes.

Decker's eyes were as old and unreadable as Milly Rood's had been that night in the San Antonio saloon more than five years ago. He sat smoking his cigar and let the three old men do the talking. That was about all they had left, waiting for the next meal and talking about things they either couldn't be a part of or wanted no part of. The world away from the hotel was a dangerous place where there didn't seem to be many happy endings. A place where the bold and reckless often had to pay a terrible price for the things they wanted. The things they wanted sometimes got them killed.

Mr. Diggs was saying in a scornful voice without ever losing his friendly smile, "She prob'ly knew so many men before she came here, she didn't even remember Tony Hill."

"Could be," Cox said, getting up to open the clanging stove door and stir up the fire with a poker. "Tony said she worked in a saloon in San Antonio for a while and then disappeared. I think he came out here lookin' for her, though he never admitted it. It was prob'ly his undoin', too."

Mr. Diggs shook his head. "I don't know why every man in this whole country gets a funny look on his face when somebody mentions Maud Hamby. Except for her hair, she ain't even pretty. Too skinny besides."

"Got a good figure though," Mr. Slocum said.

"Not compared to some I've seen," Mr. Diggs said. "I ran a clothing store in St. Louis for years and you shoulda seen some of the women who came in."

"I did see them," Mr. Slocum said. "I'm from there too, remember? Take away their bustles and corsets and padded breasts and they wouldn't have anything on Maud Hamby."

Cox still had the stove door open and nothing more important on his mind. What could be more important than heat to an old man on a cold night? The things he couldn't have no longer mattered except as things to talk about. "Think I should put in another stick?" he asked.

"I don't advise it," Mr. Diggs said. "I hear Bossy comin' now. She'll raise hell."

Cox was closing the stove door when the hotel lady appeared from the dining room, a bustling dumpy little woman in her early sixties. Gray hair framed her unsmiling round face and she scarcely needed the bustle she wore under her old dress. What she needed was to lose about half of her weight. "Good Lord, Cox! It's way too hot in here!" she cried. "I've been telling you not to waste all of my wood and that's just what I find you doing. I need you to help me in the kitchen."

"You better hire another girl, Bossy, what with all the people comin' into town because of the Apaches," Cox said, following her through the dining room toward the kitchen. "Rivera's girl ain't comin' back. That Apache grabbed her as she was walkin' home that last night we saw her."

"Oh, phooey!" the hotel lady said. "She ran off to Mexico with some no-account Mexican, that's what happened. Every time somebody sees the tracks of a unshod horse, they gallop into town and get all excited for a while and then go back home. It probably isn't even an Indian, just a wild horse. I wish somebody would catch it or shoot it."

Mr. Slocum looked toward the diminishing sound of the voices, then said in a low tone, "Seems like every time somebody sees the tracks of that unshod horse, another girl disappears. And they don't all run off to Mexico, because they ain't all Mexicans."

"Seems like they're all dark though, and pretty," Mr. Diggs said. "If Maud Hamby was a little prettier, she might need to start worryin'. She's pretty dark in spite of that tawny hair."

"Maud Hamby has got plenty to worry about without Indians," Mr. Slocum said. "Floyd Hamby will kill her someday in a fit of jealous rage."

"Why don't she leave?" Mr. Diggs asked.

"She's prob'ly afraid to. She knows he'd come after her."

"Maybe that Indian will kidnap her one of these days and Floyd will go after them and get himself ambushed," Mr. Diggs said. "This whole country would breathe easier if that man was dead."

Cole Decker decided that it *was* too hot in the lobby, as the hotel lady had said. He got up and went out on the veranda without excusing himself. That would have seemed strange in this country in the 1870s, though perhaps not to two old men who had apparently come out here from St. Louis together after one of them had found a thick roll of greenbacks lying in the street and the other one had retired. By the time they got to Rio Blanco they had probably had enough of western travel and decided to stay where there was at least a hotel. Many western towns didn't have one.

The cold wind howled down the empty street like a lonesome wolf. Eyes narrowed against the blowing dust, Decker watched a tumbleweed drift against the porch of an abandoned building. It stopped there, shivering in the wind. A tall rider on a dark horse came slowly along the street from the east. He hesitated, then drew rein near the hotel. He bent his head and cupped a match in his hands to light a cigar, and Decker recognized the dark-bearded face of Rufus Brown.

Brown shook the match out, tossed it aside, and said quietly, "Evening. I thought that was you."

Decker's voice didn't sound very friendly or trusting as he said, "You get tired of Adobe Wells?"

"I got tired of Adobe Wells the second day I was there," Brown said, glancing at the hotel. "The dining room still open?"

"They've quit serving supper. The restaurant may still be open."

"Meet me there in half an hour," Brown said. "We need to talk."

Rufus Brown rode on down the street toward the livery stable and Cole Decker headed for the restaurant. Slim Short came out of the kitchen when he heard the street door open and close. His narrow, lined face looked gaunt, old, tired, and sleepy.

"A man I know just rode into town," Decker said. "Can he get something to eat here?"

"Sure. I need the money." Short indicated the empty room.

"Fix him whatever you've got," Decker said. "He's been in the West long enough not to be too particular."

Short grunted. "He's probably been out here long enough to want a good meal. You want anything?"

"You can bring me a cup of coffee."

Short went back into the kitchen. Decker glanced about the room and then headed for a front corner table. He sat down with his back to the wall, facing the door.

Rufus Brown came in sooner than expected and took the chair opposite him, smiling sourly. "I was hoping to get here first so I could sit facing the door. But I don't guess I need to worry about my back with you sitting there."

"The man who runs the place is fixing you some supper. He should soon have it ready."

"No hurry. I'd rather talk first." He took out a fresh cigar and bit off the end. He glanced at Decker and asked, "Cigar?"

"No thanks."

Lighting his cigar, Brown watched Decker with hard dark eyes. "I closed that saloon. I'm in the bounty hunting business now. Same as you."

Decker showed no surprise. He waited.

Brown got his cigar going to his satisfaction, shook the match out and dropped it on the table. He smiled. "I know you're still in the bounty business or you wouldn't be here. You'd be long gone. But I guess you had to think about it a while. That might explain all the circling."

"I get the feeling there's something you want to tell me," Decker said.

"There is. It would be easier if we work together. But first I better explain something. The Adams bunch think I'm riding with them. They came to my place over a week ago, hot under the collar about me helping you collect the bounty on Crane. I had to do some fast talking.

"When Baldy Skall, my bartender, turned on me and asked to join up with them, I decided I'd better try to join up too, so I'd have a good excuse to stay near them."

"Where are they now?"

"Circling toward that stage station west of here. Floyd Hamby's ranch. He's their first cousin and rode with them for a while. They still use his place for a hideout and remount station. I'm supposed to meet them there."

Decker frowned but kept his thoughts to himself.

Watching him closely, Rufus Brown said, "This is no time to go soft, Decker. It could prove fatal. If you don't kill them, they'll kill you."

"Maybe I should have cleared out. Like you say, I could be long gone by now."

"That would just be putting it off. You killed two of their brothers. They'll never stop looking for you now. I figure that thought was in your head when you decided to stop here."

"Maybe."

Rufus Brown puffed his cigar thoughtfully. "Baldy Skall has got a price on his head too. He's worth eight hundred for killing two men in Santa Fe. Killed them with his bare hands when they came after him for raping their sister. He nearly killed her too. He thought she was dead, but she lived to finger him in the courtroom. After serving only a few months in the pen, he busted out, and nearly killed a couple of guards while he was doing it."

"Did you know that when you hired him?" Decker asked.

Rufus Brown shook his head, carelessly flicking ash from his cigar onto the table. "No. He didn't tell me until about a month ago, when he'd been drinking. After sobering up, he tried to deny it, but then said he'd kill anyone who tried to collect the bounty on him. I'll admit I've been thinking about it. Now I may not have any choice but to kill him. If I don't kill him, he'll kill me the first chance he gets. But I'm not sure he's got any plans to meet the others at Floyd Hamby's place. He couldn't keep his eyes off Kate Adams. He may decide to kill Mack Adams, have some fun with Kate, and then clear out. If he does, we may lose three bounties. That's rough, wild country where they were headed."

Cole Decker shifted uneasily in his chair and said nothing.

Rufus Brown smiled through his beard. "That soft spot bothering you, Decker?"

"Maybe."

Rufus Brown's smile was gone. He looked at Decker with hard eyes and said, "You're worried about that girl, even though you know she'll kill you if she gets a chance, and then prob'ly get drunk with her brothers and celebrate. She's not a nice girl, Decker. She's not a lady. She helps her brothers rob and sometimes kill people, and she seems wilder than any of them. Been that way ever since she wasn't much more than a kid, though she didn't look like one, from what I hear. A man who gets cozy with her is likely to get his throat cut and his pockets turned inside out."

Chapter 10

Cole Decker rubbed the back of his neck. "She's still a woman, and I've never shot a woman."

Rufus Brown studied him with unreadable eyes for a moment, then shrugged. "Maybe you can take her alive. But you better keep one thing in mind. A girl like her won't spend much time behind bars. She'll get out even if she has to seduce the governor, and then she'll come after you, madder than ever."

"What are you going to be doing?" Decker asked.

"I'm supposed to wait for the others at Floyd Hamby's place. I'm not going to tell him too much. I don't trust him, and he doesn't trust me. He doesn't trust anyone. But I need to nose around there and see if I can get some of his hands lined up on our side. If we have to fight them and the Adams gang too, we'll be in trouble."

"Is there a price on Floyd Hamby's head?"

"No, but there should be. If we can get his hands to testify against him, he'll soon be in jail or running from the law. He's murdered some of their friends and they've kept quiet about it out of fear. They don't want the same thing to happen to them."

"They may be afraid to turn on him."

"They are afraid, or they would have done it already. Nobody likes Floyd Hamby. But they know it's just a matter of time before some more of his men end up dead and buried in hidden graves, and they don't want it to be them. He's killed two or three of his men already."

"They could pull out."

Rufus Brown thought about that for a time. "I think I know why they don't. It's because of that woman. She seems to have a strange power over men, without even trying. I've seen her a few times. She's not the most beautiful woman I've ever seen, but when you're near her that doesn't seem to matter. I don't believe there's any way to explain it, but I figure men will be killing each other over her when she's an old lady."

"Men have been known to kill each other over women who weighed close to three hundred pounds and had about as much charm as a cow."

Rufus Brown laughed. "A lot of men like fat women. But Maud isn't fat. She's pretty tall and won't weigh more than a hundred and twenty pounds, if that much. If she worked on her appearance like some women do, she would probably be beautiful. But she doesn't seem to care how she looks. Maybe she doesn't want to look too pretty, because it would attract the attention of even more men and make Floyd even more jealous."

Rufus Brown's smile had vanished again. It never remained on his bearded face long. He seemed to be contemplating a picture in his head. By the look on his face, Decker guessed that, like so many other men, Brown had fallen victim to Maud's strange charms. He might fall victim to Floyd Hamby's jealous rage if he was not careful.

"I don't think your plan will work," Decker said. "If Floyd Hamby suspects that you're thinking about turning his men against him, he'll kill you."

"I'm not afraid of Floyd Hamby," Brown said.

"Some of his men probably wouldn't be afraid of him if he'd fight fair. But he won't. That's an advantage men like Hamby have."

Rufus Brown's dark brows were raised and the hard shine of his eyes made Decker uncomfortable. "Maybe I won't fight fair either," Brown said.

Decker shrugged with outward indifference to hide his growing doubt about Rufus Brown. He was not a man Decker could trust, but now he found himself involved in the man's schemes whether he liked it or not.

"Why don't you ride over to that little mining camp and see what you can find out," Brown suggested. "I don't need to tell you to be careful."

There were a few things that needed to be straightened out if they were going to be partners. But Cole Decker had an uneasy feeling that it did not matter. Somehow he felt sure Rufus Brown would get himself killed before he could carry out his plan to double-cross everyone who trusted him. It was very possible that he was planning to double-cross Decker if he got a chance. Decker decided it would be a good idea to put some distance between himself and Brown. Riding over to that mining camp would accomplish that, if nothing more. He got to his feet.

"I guess I'll see you later," he said, already turning away.

Rufus Brown smoked his cigar and made no reply. His dark eyes were hard and narrow as he watched Cole Decker leave the restaurant.

Decker could almost feel those eyes boring holes in his back. He was relieved when he got outside and closed the door of the restaurant behind him. The cold wind blowing along the street made him wish he could spend the night in his room at the hotel. But he doubted if he would sleep much. He needed to get away. It was better to be among enemies than around friends you couldn't trust.

A hunched figure moving through a lane of lamplight turned suspicious eyes toward Decker. He didn't know Decker and didn't trust him. It occurred to Decker that he himself had probably distrusted a lot of people who meant him no harm. But he told himself it was better to trust no one than to trust the wrong people.

The hunched figure moved away looking back over his shoulder. Decker's attention was distracted by two riders coming down the street. They were also watching Decker suspiciously from under their hat brims.

"Ain't that him?" said the slim one with the twisted face.

"Sure looks like him," said the thickset man on the stout horse.

Decker moved slowly sideways out of the light from the restaurant window, making sure his coat was unbuttoned with his left hand.

"Hey you!" the stout rider called. "Stay where you are! Get ready, Jinx!"

Out of the corner of his eye Decker saw that the stooped old man was walking faster and watching the two riders over his shoulder.

Chapter 11

The skinny one laughed and jerked out a long-barreled revolver, aiming it at Cole Decker as he spurred his horse toward the tall man in the shadows. The stout man cussed and clawed out his own gun.

Cole Decker's right hand had already sliced under his coat and reappeared gripping the stag handles of a gleaming dark .45. The gun roared and Jinx swayed from side to side until he pitched off his wild-eyed horse. Jinx hit the ground on his belly and died giggling and coughing. Cole Decker had already forgot about him and turned his gun on Tug Adams. Tug was bringing his own gun up when Cole Decker's second bullet smashed into his thick chest and pushed a loud grunt out through his open mouth.

Tug grabbed the horn of his saddle with his left hand and Decker shot him again, when he was no more than twenty feet away.

Rufus Brown stood at the door of the restaurant grinning through his beard and firing his gun at the stout man on the big horse. He thumbed off two unnecessary shots and laughed softly when the outlaw walloped the ground. The horse galloped on down the street and followed the other horse along the dark road beyond town.

"I don't think we'll have to worry about him anymore," Brown said, walking past Decker toward Tug Adams. He stopped in his tracks when the outlaw raised his head. "You still alive?"

"You barely scratched me, you double-crossin' bastard," Tug Adams said. "It was Decker who killed me. I knew we couldn't trust you. He can't either."

Rufus Brown cocked his gun and shot the dying outlaw in the head. "He was reaching for a gun."

"He dropped his gun back there," Decker said.

"I thought he was reaching for one. He's probably got a hideout."

Decker watched the bearded man in cold-eyed silence for a moment, then turned as Felix Peabody, the small old sheriff, came cautiously along the street. The sheriff was limping slightly. Perhaps he had bad feet as well as bad teeth.

"Good Lord, boy!" he said to Cole Decker. "I knew this would happen if you stayed here. Now I reckon you'll want to stay till the reward money comes back."

Decker was looking at the two dead men and did not reply.

The sheriff frowned at Rufus Brown and said, "How come you to shoot that feller when he was nearly dead already?"

"I thought he was reaching for a gun," Rufus Brown said.

The sheriff grunted. "He wasn't reachin' for no gun. I think you just wanted to shut him up. And you done a good job of it."

Rufus Brown seemed completely indifferent to the sheriff's opinion of him. He had more important things on his mind. "That's Tug Adams," he said. "He's worthy a thousand dollars dead or alive. So is Jinx. How soon can you get the money?"

"Coupla weeks, I reckon," the sheriff growled. "It's gettin' even worse. I was hopin' there wouldn't be no killin' in my town. But you led them straight here."

"They weren't following me," Brown said. "At least I don't think they were."

"They musta followed somebody," the sheriff said, glancing at Decker. "It didn't look to me like you needed no help from him. You gonna split the reward with him?"

"I guess so," Decker said. He was beginning to wish he'd never seen Rufus Brown.

There was a smug, complacent smile on Brown's face, a smile that said everything was working out even better than he had hoped. Tug and Jinx Adams lay dead in the street, the sheriff would confirm their identities from wanted posters and request the reward money, which Brown and Decker would split, a thousand dollars each.

"You still going to that stage station?" Decker asked.

Brown nodded, a worried look replacing his smile. "You may not find the others. They'll start wondering if they get there and I'm not there."

Decker doubted if that was the only reason Rufus Brown wanted to go on to the stage station.

"I doubt if they'll wonder long," the sheriff was saying. "Them two horses belonged to Floyd Hamby and they kept goin' straight toward his place."

Chapter 12

The four Circle H hands sat at a table in the bunkhouse, playing a game of cards. Their faces were silent and drawn. They were worried men, fearing their boss and not trusting each other. If they voiced their thoughts even among themselves, one of them might tell Floyd Hamby to save his own skin in a bad moment. Carl Leach, the toughest of them, had given Shorty away and they had just buried Shorty out in the desert and driven cattle back and forth over the grave so it would never be found.

A little earlier, there had been a violent quarrel at the converted ranch house, with Floyd shouting his rage and Maud yelling back at him. It had ended the way their noisy quarrels usually ended, with Floyd raping her on the floor of the big front room. They had gone on insulting each other for several minutes while it was happening, but then both of them had fallen silent.

After one of these savage matings, Floyd was usually quiet and surly for a few days, and Maud would not look at anyone. But she usually avoided looking at the hands anyway. Floyd might catch her doing it, or the one so favored might start paying too much attention to her, with tragic consequences.

The attention of the four men was not on the card game. They were all listening to the silence in the main house, and wondering if Floyd and Maud had gone to bed and were doing it again. All four hands were trying not to show their feelings. They were all in love with Maud, or maybe love was not the right word for it. They were all certainly infatuated, their heads filled with fantasies they would never talk about, even if it had been safe to do so. They were all mystified by their feelings toward Maud, for she never smiled and was not even very pretty.

Part of it, no doubt, was that she was the only woman around. It was true that there were wives and daughters at a few of the other ranches, but they were not even as pretty as Maud and the Circle H hands seldom saw them because the other ranches were so far away. Except for the dumpy and grumpy old hotel lady, there were no women at all in town. The saloon girls had been run out years ago because of the problems they caused. Several young women who had worked at the hotel had mysteriously disappeared, and the young woman who had worked briefly at the restaurant had left before the Circle H hands even knew she was there.

Bib Neeson was a nervous little puncher, no bigger than Shorty, the dead man they had buried. It was a mystery to the others why Bib had gone to work at the Circle H, or why he stayed. He nearly jumped out of his skin at every sound, and he heard every sound. He seemed to hear with his almost colorless eyes, which always started blinking and flickering before the others heard anything. Now Bib had his head in the air, listening more tensely than usual.

Then the others heard it too, the sound of approaching horses.

"That the stage?" asked Salty Jones, his eyes focused on his cards.

"Stages ain't runnin'," Paul Young said, his face pale and worried behind the peeling sunburnt skin. He seemed almost as out of place here as Bib Neeson. His eyes had been tormented at the sounds from the main house earlier, and he had listened anxiously to the silence that had followed.

Carl Leach got up and went outside as the two trotting horses turned off the road and headed for the corral. They stopped outside the corral gate. The other three hands followed Leach outside and turned their attention toward the main house, where Floyd Hamby's stout body and bearded face could be seen at the dark doorway.

"What is it?" Hamby barked.

"Two horses," Leach said. "Got saddles on them, but no riders. Looks like a couple of them you sold to Mack Adams on credit."

Hamby gave an angry bellow and headed for the corral. Leach and the other hands managed to seize the reins of the two horses before Hamby scared them away.

"It's Tug's gray and Jinx's dun!" Floyd Hamby said. "I bet Decker killed them for the bounty on their heads! He won't be satisfied till he gets us all!"

"Ain't no bounty on my head, fur as I know," Salty Jones said.

"Good," Floyd Hamby barked. "You ride into town and find out what happened."

Salty Jones sucked in a deep breath. Then without a word he pulled his hat down low over his worried eyes and saddled a horse. Minutes later he headed east along the cold windy road.

Halfway to town he saw a horse and rider coming along the road toward him at a trot. He drew rein, ready to grab his holstered gun.

"Who's that?"

A pleasant voice replied, "That's not a question you ask in this country, unless you're a greenhorn who doesn't know any better."

"I ain't no greenhorn and you better answer, mister."

The tall bearded rider trotted on toward him. "Rufus Brown. A friend of the Adams boys."

"I heard them mention you. Tug and Jinx musta run into trouble. Their horses showed up at the ranch without no riders. You know what happened to them boys?"

Rufus Brown stopped his horse ten feet away and sat relaxed in his saddle. The road was dark under a moonless sky and Salty Jones could tell nothing about the expression of Rufus Brown's bearded face. The man's eyes were hidden under the brim of his hat and that worried Salty Jones. Most of the really dangerous men he had known had an unreadable poker face, but their eyes often gave them away when they were in a fighting mood.

At last Rufus Brown said in an odd voice, "Tug and Jinx are both dead."

"Did that bounty hunter kill them?"

Rufus Brown nodded. "I'm on my way to the stage station to tell Hamby now. I was supposed to meet Mack and Kate and my bartender, Baldy Skall, there. Me and Baldy have joined up with them. Mack needed a couple of men after Decker killed Crane and Tip. Have Mack and them arrived yet?"

"We ain't seen them." Salty Jones started to glance back over his shoulder, then decided to keep his eyes on Rufus Brown. "Floyd Hamby ain't too sociable and he don't trust nobody he don't know."

"I've stopped at his place a few times. He'll remember me."

"Well, you can talk to him. But don't be surprised if he runs you off."

"Mack Adams wouldn't like that."

Salty Jones grinned. "Floyd does a lot of things folks don't like. I better ride back with you. I ain't got no reason to go on to town now, and he wouldn't like it if I did."

Salty turned his horse around and he and Rufus Brown rode side by side along the road toward the ranch and stage station.

"You like working for Hamby?" Rufus Brown asked.

Salty Jones laughed. It was not a pleasant laugh. Salty Jones was not a pleasant man, nor one Rufus Brown felt he could trust. Jones said, "I don't like nothin' about workin' for Floyd Hamby. But don't tell him I said that."

"I won't." Rufus Brown rode in silence for a few minutes, watching the dark brush and rocks that seemed to be watching him from both sides of the road. Then he glanced at Salty Jones and asked, "Ever wonder what it would be like at the ranch without Floyd Hamby?"

Salty Jones grinned.

CHAPTER 13

The lone Indian had captured girls before—mostly Apaches and Mexicans, a few white girls—but never one like Kate Adams.

Even with her hands bound with rawhide strips behind her back and her ankles bound together, she fought him. When he tried to mount her in the dark cave, she butted him in the face and brought her knees up into his groin, nearly unmanning him.

Now he let her alone and crouched near the mouth of the cave. He occasionally turned his head toward her dim shape near the back of the cave, but mostly he watched the faint trail that wound through the brush of the narrow valley and up the rocky slope to the cave.

He gripped his Spencer in his right hand with the butt plate against the ground. He had hid the girl's cartridge belt and empty holster in the cave. Her pistol had been lost in the first struggle with him.

He had gagged her to keep her quiet, but he knew she was wide awake and watching him with her dark eyes. She looked more like a Mexican than a white girl, but she did not speak Mexican. He spoke the Mexican tongue but knew only a little English.

Now he had to decide what to do about her. If he kept her captive, she would try to get loose and kill him somehow. But he could not free her and he hated to kill her. She was a beautiful animal, just what he wanted.

Of course, sooner or later he would kill her, as he had killed all the others. A man like him could not always be fettered with a female.

Sometimes he killed one he was tired of so he would be free to look for a new one. There was nothing like the excitement he felt when stalking his next lovely victim.

But with this one, he felt like a victim himself, and it was not a feeling he liked.

He needed to check on the two horses tethered a piece from the cave and make sure no one was around. But first he wanted to make sure the girl hadn't loosened her bonds. Without a doubt, she had been trying to, taking advantage of the darkness in the cave and knowing his eyes would be affected by the light outside. Though dim, it seemed almost as bright as day compared to the blackness inside the cave.

He turned and rose in one easy movement. Feeling and testing the cave floor through his moccasins, he made no sound as he went toward her, coming in cautiously from her right side. Too late he realized something was wrong. He had left her lying on her left side with her hands tied behind her back. Now she lay flat on her back. As he leaned over, she moved suddenly. Her freed right hand came up holding a rock and swung it at his head.

The rock seemed to explode against his forehead and he fell sideways, dropping the rifle. Lying stunned on the cave floor, he was dimly aware of her sitting up and struggling with the rawhide binding her ankles. Then she was feeling on the ground for the rifle.

He managed to get his knife out and slashed desperately at her. She scrambled back out of reach, grunting and cussing. Then she got up and ran from the cave as he groped for the rifle. He heard her running down the rough, rocky slope toward the narrow valley below.

He doubted if she would find the horses. He had hidden them in a little pocket of grass behind some tall brush and rocks after bringing her to the cave.

He should have killed her, he told himself. Now, dazed and staggering from the blow to his forehead and half blinded by the blood trickling into his eyes, he would have to hunt her down. He dared not let her get away. She had got a good look at him and would be able to identify him if she ever saw him again.

Anyone who saw his face had to die. That was the only way he could stay alive.

Floyd Hamby scowled across the long plank table at Rufus Brown.

There was no one else in the big room. The woman called Maud was keeping out of sight in the kitchen and making no sound that could be heard. She had brought Rufus Brown a cup of coffee and turned away without looking at him or saying anything.

Floyd Hamby cleared his throat and said in his harsh voice, "You claim the whole Adams bunch was headed here, but you're the only one who has arrived. Seems kind of odd."

"He told me to come along the road, which is shorter than the route they took," Brown said, glancing down at the strong black coffee in his cup. "I'm not sure why Tug and Jinx decided to come through Rio Blanco."

"Why didn't you give them a hand with Decker?"

"By the time I got out on the street it was over and that old sheriff was standing there. So there was nothing I could do. I heard Decker tell him he was going to ride over to that old mining town looking for the others. He figured that was where they'd gone, since they weren't with Tug and Jinx. And he guessed right. That's where Mack and Kate and Baldy Skall were headed, like I told you. But I figured they'd come on here if they didn't find Decker there."

"They'll prob'ly spend the night there," Floyd Hamby said, getting to his feet. "Let's ride over there and give them a hand. Make sure that bastard gets what he deserves."

"You taking your men with you?"

"I'll take Leach and Jones. Them other two wouldn't be no help in a fight."

"I'm surprised you keep men like them around," Rufus Brown said.

Floyd Hamby glared at him with bloodshot eyes. "I keep them around because they do whatever I tell them to do. They're afraid not to."

The woman appeared at the kitchen door and stood there watching Hamby. He shifted his scowl to her and said, "If Mack and them get here before I get back, tell them to wait here."

The woman made no reply. She was still careful not to look at Rufus Brown, but he could not resist the impulse to look at her, though he knew Floyd Hamby was glaring suspiciously at him.

The woman was just as slim as he remembered, but that only made her curves more noticeable, even under the old gray dress she wore. Her hair was almost blond on top, but darker lower down. Her eyes seemed to be no particular color, but a shade that suggested several different colors—gray and green and hazel, but darker in poor light. He guessed she was in her late twenties.

One thing puzzled him. Her eyes were direct and fearless when she looked at Floyd Hamby, but she avoided eye contact with other men around Hamby. Maybe she just wanted to avoid trouble. Brown didn't believe she was afraid of Hamby or afraid to leave him. She stayed with the harsh, insanely jealous man for some other reason.

Perhaps she found his jealousy flattering and his violent anger exciting. Many women seemed to find danger exciting.

Perhaps she was even in love with the hairy brute! Rufus Brown found that thought unacceptable and he immediately rejected it. He had suspected for quite a while that she only stayed here because she knew it was only a matter of time before Hamby got himself killed, and then all he owned would be hers. Since she didn't seem afraid of the man, that was the only thing that made sense.

"You ready, Brown?" Hamby asked impatiently.

Rufus Brown looked down at his coffee cup, then pushed it away and got to his feet. It gave him a secret feeling of satisfaction when he noticed that he was a good two inches taller than Hamby. He was not as powerfully built as Hamby, but that scarcely mattered in a country where men usually did their fighting with guns and let their horses do all the heavy work.

"I'll need a fresh horse," Brown said. "I hope you can loan me one."

There was a savage gleam in Hamby's small eyes. "You can take Shorty's. He won't need it anymore."

That meant Shorty was dead, and Rufus Brown considered it bad luck to ride a dead man's horse. But he only nodded. A wrong word now might ruin everything.

Being so unsure of Maud's feelings, he wanted no trouble with Floyd Hamby here.

He wanted Hamby to die somewhere else, not knowing—until the last moment—who was responsible for his death.

Chapter 14

Baldy Skall had got hold of himself and decided that the danger was probably not as great as he had thought at first. Like most people who had spent much time in their country, he had an almost superstitious terror of Apaches. He knew his bull strength would be of little use against their ghostly movements and sadistic methods. But he believed there was only one Apache around, and that was the one who made a practice of kidnapping attractive young women who were never seen again, though strange tales sometimes drifted back of this one or that one having been seen somewhere. It was unlikely that the Indian, with a wildcat like Kate Adams on his hands, would try to hunt Skall down.

The night was dark, windy, and scary, the country strange to him. He spent most of the night riding around in circles, not knowing where he was or where he was going. It would probably be a mistake to try to find his way to Floyd Hamby's place and make contact with Rufus Brown, Tug and Jinx Adams. He didn't trust Brown and the other two didn't trust him. And what if Kate managed to escape from the Indian and made her way to the Hamby ranch and stage station? She would have a story to tell that would contradict the one Baldy Skall had been fabricating in his head and sometimes rehearsing aloud, to see how it would sound. He somehow knew they would believe her story, not his. Her anger and outrage would convince them.

No, it would be best to go somewhere else, strike out on his own.

But wherever he went, he would need a stake.

Dawn found him back at the spot where he had killed Mack Adams and begun his fruitless pursuit of Kate. He stopped his big horse and gazed at the body of the dead man, at first with resentment. He felt almost betrayed. It looked like killing Mack Adams would cause him a lot of trouble and it hadn't got him what he wanted, which was Kate.

But it suddenly occurred to him that here might be a solution to one of his problems. Mack Adams was worth $1500, dead or alive. That was a lot of money. The problem was how to collect it.

Then he remembered that Cole Decker had sold the body of Crane Decker to Rufus Brown. Brown had voluntarily paid him the full market price for the body of the wanted outlaw because of a favor Decker had once done him. No one owed Baldy Skall anything but a bullet, but maybe he could sell Mack Adams's body to someone for a thousand or twelve hundred dollars. That would be better than taking the dead outlaw to some lawman's office himself and run the risk of getting arrested. Any lawman worth his salary was likely to remember reading Baldy Skall's description or seeing his ugly face on a wanted poster.

Skall remembered where he, Mack, and Kate had been headed—that old mining camp whose name apparently changed so often nobody could be sure what name it was currently using. Maybe someone there had enough money to buy the dead outlaw from him in the hope of turning a tidy profit.

First, Skall got down to examine the body. The shotgun blast had messed up the outlaw's back pretty bad, but the smell of dead meat had drawn no prowling animals to the feast yet. That was a relief. Baldy had seen dead men with most of their faces eaten away. Mack's face was undamaged and his dark eyes were wide open in surprise. Identification should be no problem.

Skall loaded the heavy body on his own horse, and then, leading the horse, he went looking for Mack's horse. He found the horse, still saddled, grazing on a bald ridge. The alert horse raised his head to watch Baldy approach with his big hand out in a friendly gesture, talking softly to sooth the animal, making promises he didn't mean to keep.

Skall was soon on his way, riding Mack's fine horse and leading his own corpse-laden animal along the trail to the old mining camp. So far everything was going better than he had expected.

It was late morning when he saw the first shacks of the mining camp. Some of the old buildings were boarded up, others simply abandoned. Only a few of the buildings in the center of the camp appeared to be occupied. It was a bad sign. Baldy had sensed that things were going too well and that the bad luck of yesterday would soon return.

He saw the familiar batwing doors of a saloon and turned that way with his big teeth bared in a hopeful grin. He felt at home in saloons, having spent so much of his adult life in them, as a customer, bouncer, or bartender.

He paid no attention to the single horse tied at the rail in front of the saloon. All horses looked a lot alike to him. He had never ridden one until he was past thirty.

Tying his horses beside the other one, he decided to leave his shotgun on the saddle. He pulled his pants up a little over his huge belly, adjusted his big hat, and swaggered into the saloon. There was a bigger crowd in the place than he had expected, after seeing the nearly deserted town. Bearded men sat at tables and a few others stood at the bar. A tall lean man who had no beard stood at the bar, his back to Baldy Skall. He wore a black hat and coat. Baldy didn't notice what kind of pants he wore. But he was about the only one in the small saloon who didn't turn his head to see who had come in and there was no back-bar mirror, so Baldy guessed the man wasn't interested in him and therefore posed no threat.

Baldy stopped just inside the swing doors and asked in a loud voice, "Anybody interested in makin' some money real easy?"

One of the bearded miners or prospectors laughed. "I reckon everybody's interested in easy money. Who you want killed?"

"Any law here?" Baldy asked.

"No law allowed," said a grinning, well-dressed man with a black beard but no hair on his head. He was the only man in the place who wore no hat. He was almost as broad as he was tall. "I'm Duff Lumpkin. I own this place. The men you see here are about the only ones left in this camp, and most of them will prob'ly leave if they ever sober up. What was it you said about easy money?"

Baldy drew a deep breath and had trouble speaking calmly. He was suddenly almost overcome by the memory of his ordeal in the desert, even though he had brought it on himself when he killed Mack Adams and caused Kate to get captured by a savage Indian. All that went through his mind as he said, "Me and Mack Adams

and his sister Kate were headed this way when we was attacked by
Apaches. The truth is, I think there was only one and all he wanted
was that girl. I was ready to blast him with my shotgun, but Mack
rode in front of me and I hit him instead.

"Kate took off with that Indian right behind her. I chased him a
piece, but both him and Kate got way ahead of me and I went back to
see if Mack was still alive. He was dead and I spent the night lookin'
for Kate and that Indian. But I never found them."

"You want some help lookin' for them?" Lumpkin asked.

Baldy shook his head. "I think it would be a waste of time. And I
need to get outta the country. I'm wanted by the law and so was Mack
Adams. It seems like a pity to let fifteen hundred dollars go to waste.
That's the price on Mack's head. But if I tried to collect it, I'd prob'ly
get arrested my own self."

Everyone in the saloon laughed except the tall lean man who kept
his back to Baldy.

"So what have you got in mind?" Lumpkin asked, still smiling
with his almost colorless eyes.

"I've got Mack's body outside on a horse. I'd like to sell him for
twelve hundred dollars. That's three hundred less'n he's worth. But
I want real money. I never could tell gold dust from any other kinda
dirt, and I don't want to find out too late that I been swindled outta
twelve hundred dollars."

"Afraid you're outta luck," Lumpkin said, watching Baldy with
his strange pale eyes. "I'm the only one in this camp who's got that
kinda cash, and I wouldn't give you more than a thousand for him."

The tall lean man turned and looked at Baldy through cold gray
eyes. "I might take him off your hands."

Baldy tensed. The tall man was Cole Decker.

"I ain't doin' no kinda business with you!" Baldy said, backing
toward the door. "I know who you are! You already killed two of the
Adams boys!"

"Four," Cole Decker said. "And I'll kill you if you don't do like I
say. You're going to take me to the place where you killed Mack Adams."

"Now hold on a minute," Lumpkin said. "Me and this big feller
were talkin' business. I don't care what the two of you do afterwards.
But wait till me and him see if we can make a deal." He shifted his
eyes back to Baldy Skall. "I'll give you a thousand dollars for Mack
Adams's carcass, if it's really him. And I'll know, because I've seen

posters with his face on them."

"It's him and it's a deal," Baldy said. "I'll throw in the horse he's on, even though it was mine before I decided to trade with him."

There was more coarse, drunken laughter in the saloon.

It was an hour past noon when Baldy Skall drew rein and pointed his thick trigger finger.

"It happened right here. Kate Adams took off down that way with that Indian chasin' her."

"You sure it wasn't you chasing her?" Cole Decker asked. He got down off his horse and walked ahead a piece to study the tracks on the ground, ignoring Baldy Skall's whining assertion that he was a good ole country boy and he wouldn't do nothin' like that.

Baldy Skall fell silent and stared at Decker's exposed back in disbelief. Decker had not taken Baldy's guns and now he was turning his back to a man no one in their right mind had trusted since he was a baby. In the saloon in that old mining camp, when all the others were laughing and looking at one another, Decker had kept his cold watchful eyes on Baldy Skall. But now, when there were no witnesses and Decker should have kept his eyes on Baldy, he turned his back like a dumb greenhorn.

Baldy could scarcely believe his luck. His lethal shotgun hung from the saddle horn by a loop of leather rein tied around the small part of the stock. It would take too long to lift the shotgun, cock the hammer and aim the weapon. Baldy decided to use the ivory-handled Colt that had belonged to Kate Adams. He was reaching for the Peacemaker when Cole Decker suddenly turned and looked at him with those cold gray eyes.

Baldy Skall didn't see the lean man draw the gun that roared in his fist. And Skall scarcely felt the bullet that tore a small red hole in his massive chest. He had been punched harder by men half his size. He was puzzled at the weak numbness spreading over him. The white-handled gun fell out of his hand and then he was falling out of the saddle.

A horse exploded from the brush and rocks and Decker saw Floyd Hamby's scowling bearded face behind the big pistol in Hamby's hand. Before Decker could swing his gun toward Hamby, three other riders appeared behind the man. Rufus Brown brought up the rear. He fired past two bewildered looking riders and Floyd Hamby grunted in surprise and then swayed drunkenly out of the saddle, his gun unfired.

The two riders behind Hamby were gazing at him in wonder when two more shots knocked them off their running horses.

Cole Decker hadn't fired at anyone but Baldy Skall. He held a cocked gun in his hand and watched Rufus Brown ride out of the brush grinning through his beard and casually reloading his own gun.

"You can't say you got them all this time," he said happily.

"Looks like you got them all, except your friend Baldy," Decker said.

"That double-crossing fat bastard was no friend of mine," Rufus Brown said. He looked at the cocked gun in Decker's hand, then holstered his own gun. He watched closely until Decker eased the hammer down on his gleaming dark revolver and put it back in the holster. Then Brown smiled with relief, bit off the end of a cigar and looked at the four dead men. "Too bad none of them's worth anything except Baldy Skall. I heard what he said about Kate Adams. Think he was telling the truth?"

"I don't know."

"But you intend to find out," Rufus Brown said with a thin, twisted version of his smile. "By the way, is Mack dead?"

"Yes. Skall sold his body to a man in that old mining town for a thousand dollars. It's in his pocket."

Rufus Brown thought for a moment, rubbing his bearded chin. "Tell you what. You take the money. I'll take Baldy in and collect the reward on him. I'll put the other three on their horses and take them to the stage station and tell Maud they were killed by Apaches. I doubt if she'll believe me, but I don't think she'll care."

"You could be wrong."

"I don't think so. I figure she's been hoping Hamby would get himself killed so she could inherit his ranch and stage station. I'll give you another thousand and then I'll collect for Tug and Jinx Adams. Is that agreeable?"

"All right."

Brown smiled again. "I thought so. It may take a while, since the stages have quit running. And you want to find Kate Adams and that Indian. You better be careful. She'll put a bullet in you if she gets a chance."

Decker didn't say anything.

The Indian waited near the two horses. He was growing impatient, though it didn't show on his rocklike face. The girl should have appeared by now. She had probably guessed that he was watching the horses and she might have decided to walk out of the desert, though he considered that unlikely. The Mexicans and the whites didn't want to go anywhere without a horse to ride.

He believed that if she came at all, he would be able to spot her some distance off and watch her approach through the rocks and brush. But it didn't happen that way. She just stepped out of the brush into the open space where the two horses were. She looked carefully about with her dark eyes and then moved toward the Appaloosa.

The Apache stepped into the open also, because he wanted her to see him and know who killed her. Her dark eyes flashed with fear and hatred as he raised the rifle.

The bullet struck him in the right temple and he spun around and fell, dropping the rifle.

Kate looked at the dead Indian in surprise, and then her eyes searched the rocks and brush. After several long minutes Cole Decker appeared near the motionless Indian with a pistol in his hand. His black coat was unbuttoned and Kate saw her ivory-handled Colt stuck in his waistband.

He made sure the Indian was dead, then holstered his gun and got the Spencer rifle. He looked at the rifle and then broke it on a rock.

"You bastard!" Kate said. "I think I'd rather be dead than to be rescued by you."

Cole Decker looked at her with his lonely eyes, then reached for the ivory-handled Colt and tossed it to her. "It's not loaded," he said.

"I should have known!" she said, her mouth twisting with sarcasm. "But I know where he put my shell belt and I won't waste any time gettin' it!"

"Good luck," Decker said, turning his back on her.

"You're the one who'll need it! Don't think you can get away with killin' two of my brothers!"

"Four," Cole Decker said without looking back. "I killed four of them. All of your brothers are dead."

The girl screamed her grief and rage, then yelled, "You better kill me while you've got a chance!"

"I can't," Cole Decker said.

The girl looked after him with puzzled, anguished eyes. Then she looked at the dead Indian who would have killed her if Cole Decker hadn't killed him first.

Then she sat down and cried, but not for long.

She decided to go after Cole Decker anyway. She couldn't let him get away. But she was no longer sure why she wanted to prevent his escape.

She kept thinking about what a tall, fine-looking man he was.

CHAPTER 15

Maud opened the door as soon as she heard the walking horses stop in front of it. Rufus Brown was biting off the end of a slender cigar. The other three horses were tied behind his. The body of a dead man was tied across the saddle of each horse. She gazed at the body of Floyd Hamby without speaking.

Half smiling, Rufus Brown studied her with interest. She had put on a different dress and done something to her face and hair. He could scarcely believe the transformation. He was looking at a very attractive woman and he told himself she had made herself look that way for him. She had somehow known that Floyd Hamby wouldn't come back alive.

"Apaches got them," Rufus Brown said casually, still studying her with a half smile on his bearded face.

She was watching him closely now. Her face didn't change, but there was a look in her eyes that worried him. He couldn't see her right hand and that also made him uneasy.

"How is it you made it back without a scratch?" she asked in a cold hard tone.

"I stayed behind a rock and kept shooting till the Apaches left," he said.

"How many were there?" she asked.

"I'm not sure. They stayed out of sight in the rocks."

"That's what you should have done," she said. "You shouldn't have come back here with a story like that."

She brought her right hand up and there was a gun in it. She cocked the gun and shot Rufus Brown off the horse.

Paul Young and Bib Neeson came around the corner of the house and stopped in their tracks, their scared eyes darting from the gun in her hand to the dead man she had just shot.

"Get the others down, then ride into town and tell that old sheriff that they were all killed by Apaches." She looked at the two frightened hands and added, "If you boys do like you're told, you'll be rewarded for helping me and for your silence."

Scarcely able to believe what they knew she meant, the two shaky hands stuttered incoherently and got busy obeying her orders.

Cole Decker crossed the stage road and headed east across some cattleman's unfenced range. He was in no hurry and he took his time, riding at a slow trot and sometimes at a walk.

He came to a waterhole surrounded by better grass than he usually saw in this country. There were close to fifty head of horny range cattle grazing near the waterhole. Most of them wore the late Floyd Hamby's Circle H brand, although this was pretty far from the ranch house he had also used as a stage station.

Decker dismounted and filled his canteen while the dark chestnut drank. He tried not to think about all the cows and coyotes and other animals that had slobbered and maybe done worse things in the muddy looking water. It had been a long time since he had drunk any water that he trusted, but so far none of it had killed him.

Kate Adams seemed determined to correct that mistake or whatever it was. She rode up on her beautiful Appaloosa with a beautiful pistol in her hand. The gun was cocked and aimed directly at Decker. But she had some things to tell him before she pulled the trigger. Decker had already heard some of it.

She wore a man's shirt and her tight jeans and no hat to hide any of her beautiful black hair or her beautiful tan face.

"You're dead now, Decker!" she told him. "I told you you couldn't get away with killin' all of my brothers!"

"I only killed four of them!"

Her dark eyes flashed. "That's four too many!"

"They were trying to kill me. What would you have done in my place?"

Kate Adams bit her thin but pretty lips. "I've been thinkin' about that. In your place, I woulda got mad as hell and prob'ly shot all of my brothers except Mack and Crane. They were the only ones I ever cared about. I never much liked Tug and I couldn't stand Jinx.

"What about Tip?"

She flushed. "I couldn't stand Tip most of the time either. But I was a little in love with him, even though he was my brother. Before you killed him, I was alone with him a lot when we split up. It was usually Mack and Tug, Crane and Jinx, and me and Tip. I think Mack figured out what was goin' on and he started keepin' me and Tip separated. But I don't know what he expected, since he made sure I never saw any men except my brothers."

"I think I better not ask any more questions about Tip."

"No, you better not," she said. "Get away from that horse, then unbuckle your gun belt and toss it over here."

Decker silently obeyed, never taking his worried eyes off the girl.

"Now take off your coat and turn all the way around. Toss the coat over here by your gun belt." When he obeyed, she got off the Appaloosa and bent down to run her left hand over the coat while keeping her gun pointed at the tall man. She found his wallet and placed her gun on his coat long enough to open the wallet and look at the greenbacks in it. "It's mine now, Decker. You won't need it anymore. I think I'll keep your coat too. It gets cold at night."

"There are other ways to keep warm."

"I've been thinkin' about that," she said. She studied him silently for a moment. "Take off the rest of your clothes."

He glanced uneasily about. "In front of all those cows?"

"The cows won't bother you, Decker. I'm the one you better be worried about."

"What have you got in mind?"

"Guess." She holstered her gun, unbuckled her gun belt and dropped it on his coat. Then she began taking off her clothes. "I keep rememberin' that you saved my life, Decker. I ain't decided what I'm gonna do yet—or what I'm gonna do about you. But I'm glad I'm not dead. I'm only nineteen years old and I want to do a lot of livin' before I die. While I'm tryin' to decide what to do about you, we can keep each other warm at night."

"It's not night. It's broad daylight. And those damn cows keep looking over this way and rolling their eyes at us."

"Forget about them old cows, Decker. I'm the one you better be thinkin' about."

After Decker saw her standing there naked, he said no more about the cows.

Excerpt from
The Hell Riders
by Van Holt

No one ever knew for certain what his name was. Somebody remarked that he
looked a lot like another stranger, named Gatten, who had been killed in the
Last Chance Saloon the year before. So Gatten he was called. The bartender
at the Last Chance Saloon supplied a first name when he called him John.
The bartender, Carl Lewis, called everyone John, since he could not remember
anyone's name.

The stranger appeared in the weather-beaten plank town one cold windy
afternoon when dust obscured the gray walls of mountains bordering the
sage plain in every direction. A tall gaunt looking man with dark blond hair
and cold gray eyes, he paused to knock dust from his somber black clothes
before entering the Travelers Hotel. A short time before, he had ridden in
out of the haze of dust-filtered sunlight and left his dark horse at the livery
stable.

When Hal Chaney pushed the register toward him, the stranger frowned
as if irritated, but said nothing. After a noticeable hesitation, he picked up
the pen, made an "X" in the heavy book, and pushed it back toward the ho-
telkeeper.

Hal Chaney studied the "X" in silence for a moment. He felt certain that
the stranger could have signed his name if he had wanted to. But for some

he did not want his name known and did not want to sign any other name in the hotel register. Carefully avoiding the stranger's frosty gray eyes, Chaney handed him a key and said, "Take number 2. It's over the street." Somehow he knew the stranger would want a room overlooking the street.

The stranger silently climbed the stairs with his saddlebags and blanket roll. Standing at the window of his room a short time later, he saw a buckboard coming along the street, a tall black man of about thirty handling the lines. On the seat beside him sat a woman with a beautiful white face and long dark hair. The stranger's frosty gray eyes glittered as he watched them.

Standing at the door of the Last Chance Saloon, Chet Mullen said over his shoulder, "How long we gonna let that go on, Buff?"

An unshaved, tawny-haired man with bright yellowish eyes peered at him from a table near the front of the saloon. "What?" he asked.

"Her and that black rascal that she wants us to call Cookie, like she does. Got Colonel Easton to say he'd fire anyone who calls him what I'd like to call him. They just drove up to the general store."

There were two other men sitting at the table besides Buff Cooger. They got up at once and strolled to the batwings, leaving Cooger sitting there by himself, his catlike eyes slowly blinking through the tawny hair that fell over them. "Long as the old man tells us to, I reckon," he said. "She's got him twisted around her little finger."

"You think he knows what's goin' on?" Mullen asked.

"Hell, he must," Cooger said. "He may be crippled, but he ain't blind or deaf."

"Here comes that stranger who just rode into town," Moss Tuggle said. "He looks familiar, don't he?"

"He sure as hell does," Chet Mullen agreed, as he and the other two sauntered back to the table where Cooger sat. "I've seen him somewhere before, or somebody who looked a lot like him."

When the tall man in black entered the saloon from the windy street, he seemed not to notice the four men sitting at the table, watching him with sharp, suspicious eyes. He stepped up to the bar, and Carl Lewis asked the question he always asked.

"What'll it be, John?"

The stranger glanced at him in wonder, then said briefly, in a soft voice that barely reached the four rough-garbed men at the table, "Whiskey."

"Bad day out," the short swarthy bartender said as he uncorked a bottle and poured the stranger's drink. He glanced toward the street and continued to talk about the weather while the stranger sipped his whiskey, but the stranger did not seem to hear him. No one paid much attention to Carl Lewis, but he seemed happily unaware of their indifference.

The four men at the table continued to study the stranger with hostile eyes. They noticed that he wore two guns, one in his waistband, the other in a tied-down holster. The guns made them uneasy, for he looked like he knew how to use them.

The stranger paid for his drink and stepped to the batwings as the buckboard made a sharp turn on the dusty street and left town, the black man urging the two horses into a fast trot.

"Come back again, John," the bartender said.

The stranger went out without answering.

Moss Tuggle, a stout red-faced young man in his twenties, rose from his chair and strode up to the bar.

"What'll it be, John?" the bartender asked.

"You know that man from someplace?" Tuggle asked, scowling.

The smiling bartender shook his head. "Never saw him before in my life."

Tuggle grunted and went back to the table with a fresh bottle.

"He calls everybody John," Kute Hurley said, grinning.

"I know I've seen him somewhere," Tuggle said, uncorking the bottle.

Buff Cooger was studying the batwing doors through which the stranger had recently gone. "You know," he said slowly, "he looked a lot like that fellow who come in here back last year."

The other three turned sharp eyes on him. "Which one?"

"You know."

There was a moment of silence.

Then Chet Mullen exclaimed, "Oh, that one! That feller called Gatten, who said a saloon wasn't the place to mention a lady."

Kute Hurley bared his yellow teeth in a wet grin. "Lady, hell," he said.

"Think he could be Gatten's brother?" Moss Tuggle asked in a worried tone.

Buff Cooger slowly nodded. "That's my guess."

There was another silence. Then Tuggle asked, "Think he knows?"

Cooger shrugged his round shoulders, his shaggy head bent forward as usual. "Could be. There's a lot of talkers in this town, like everywhere."

"Hell, he never even so much as glanced at us," Chet Mullen said.

"That don't mean nothin'. Some men look without seein', and some see without lookin'."

"Quick trip," Colonel Easton said, watching her from his wheelchair.

She turned and stood with her back to him, looking through the window at the tall black man who was unloading supplies from the buckboard. "I saw him," she said.

"Saw who?" Colonel Easton asked.

"The last man on earth I ever wanted to see again," she said. "He looked right through me with those cold gray eyes and walked on down the street as if he hadn't seen me. But he saw me all right."

"You sure it was him?" Colonel Easton asked.

She nodded. "It's him."

"Damn," Colonel Easton said softly, running a trembling hand trough his thin white hair. "After all these years." Then, after a lengthy silence, he asked, "How did he look?"

Her long dark lashes narrowed in a puzzled frown. "Different somehow. Just older, I guess."

The old man watched her with bitter eyes, trying in vain to control the trembling that always betrayed him when he was reminded of an old frustrated rage that had consumed him. "I knew he'd find us sooner or later, even in this godforsaken desert. I'm surprised it took him so long. Been ten years since the war ended. Longer than that since—"

She turned without looking at him and left the room to keep from hearing the rest. She had heard it before. She left the house and headed for the one-room shack where the black cook stayed by himself. He looked up with wide eyes when the door creaked open. He was hurriedly loading a huge old pistol that looked so rusty the woman doubted if it would even shoot. She doubted if he knew how to shoot it.

"What do you think you're doing?" she asked.

"I am gonna kill him befo' he kill me," the black man said excitedly. "I know why he here."

"Don't be a fool. He'll kill you."

"He won't kill me neither," the black man said. "I'm gonna kill him first."

"You're a fool," she said scornfully. "You can't kill that man."

"A bullet will kill him same as anybody else," Cookie said, his long dark fingers trembling as he fumbled cartridges into the converted Dragoon Colt.

The man called John Gatten cleaned his gleaming dark revolvers with very sure, steady hands and put one of them under the pillow. His gun belt, with the other pistol in the holster, now hung on the bedpost. Then he blew out the light and crawled into bed, having cleaned up and eaten supper earlier in the dining room downstairs. The blond waitress was tall and slender and shapely, but had avoided his eyes and had exchanged only a few words with him—possibly because the hotel man, Hal Chaney, had kept his eye on her. Perhaps she was Chaney's wife, although Gatten had seen no ring on her finger. He thought about her for a moment, and then his thoughts returned, inevitably, to the dark-haired woman he had seen in the buckboard, sitting beside the black man.

The frame building creaked in the wind. But after a time it seemed to him that most of the creaking came from the narrow balcony outside his window. It sounded like the boards were creaking under the weight of a man moving slowly and cautiously toward his window. His right hand went under the pillow and closed on the smooth walnut butt of the Smith & Wesson .44 Russian.

A moment later he saw the motionless shadow of a man on the window curtain. Not only that, he could see the shadow of the huge pistol that the man held in his hand. He lifted the Smith & Wesson and began firing, shattering the night silence with the roar of the gun and the sound of breaking glass. The man screamed and fell off the balcony, carrying the rail with him and crashing to the street below. A moment later Gatten heard him running off down the alley, still yelling. He could tell it was the black man.

They could hear the black man yelling something even before they heard the pounding hoofs of the horse. Moments later the door burst open and he stood there, his clothes covered with blood, his eyes wild.

"He kill me! He kill me!" he cried. "Oh, Lawd, I'm dyin'!"

"Get that black rascal out of here!" Colonel Easton yelled, trying to rise from his wheelchair.

"He's been hurt," she said, going toward the moaning negro.

"I don't care if he's dyin'!" Colonel Easton screamed. "I don't want him in my house! I've told you a hundred times!"

She helped the wounded man to the one-room shack between the main house and the bunkhouse, made him sit down in a chair, cut off the blood-soaked shirt, got hot water and whiskey and washed and bandaged his wounds, none of them very serious. All the while he kept taking on and saying that he was going to die.

"Get hold of yourself," she told him. "You're not even badly hurt. But it's a wonder you're not dead. The next time he'll kill you."

The black man rolled his eyes in horror. "Ain't gonna be no next time! I done learnt my lesson!"

She heard the hands returning and helped Cookie get into his bed. Then she stepped outside, peering at the riders as they halted in the dark yard. She could not see them clearly, but in her mind she could see Buff Cooer's catlike yellow eyes blinking back at her from under his shaggy brows.

"Did Cookie make it back?" Cooger asked.

She nodded, her green eyes cold in the dark. She did not like him or the tone of his voice. None of them bothered to remove their hats—that was how little they respected her. "He's inside," she said. "He's been shot up pretty bad."

Just then Colonel Easton yelled, "Cooger! Buff Cooger! Want a word with you!"

Cooger dropped lightly to the ground like a big lazy cat, handed his reins to one of the others and strolled into the main house. "You want to see me, Colonel?"

The old man's pale blue eyes were a little wild. His hands griped the arms of his wheelchair and his knuckles were white. His voice shook when he spoke. "You see the man who shot that black rascal?"

Cooger nodded. "He looked a lot like that man we killed in town about a year back. Gatten or something like that. I never was sure what his name was."

"Never mind who he is," the old Colonel said bitterly. "I know who he is. What I wanted to ask you, when do you expect Mac and them other boys back?"

"In a day or two, I guess. I figgered they'd be back before now."

"You don't think they run into no trouble, do you?"

"I doubt it. They prob'ly just decided to celebrate a little before they come back."

"Well, you other boys stay close by," Colonel Easton said. "I may need you."

"Gatten?" Buff Cooger asked.

Colonel Easton nodded, the bitterness returning to his watery blue eyes. "If that's what you want to call him."

The young woman came in as Buff Cooger was leaving. He looked at her through his catlike eyes, but she did not even glance at him, keeping her attention on the white-haired old man in the wheelchair. "He needs a doctor," she said, as the door closed behind Cooger.

Colonel Easton turned his bitter eyes on her. "You're more worried about that black rascal than you are about me," he said accusingly.

"It was your idea to come here," she reminded him. "I told you we should go someplace where there was a good doctor."

"I did it for you!" Colonel Easton said. "I hoped against hope he wouldn't find us in a godforsaken place like this. But now he's here, and after that black rascal tried to kill him too—he'll prob'ly think we put him up to it! If there was ever any hope of talkin' him out of whatever he's got planned, we can forget about it now! Now it's either him or us!"

The preceding was from the gritty western novel
The Hell Riders

To keep reading, click or go here:
http://amzn.to/1haTsFq

Excerpt from
The Revenge of Tom Graben
(sequel to The Return of Frank Graben) by Van Holt

Frank Graben stopped his blue roan gelding among some rocks on a bleak barren ridge top and studied the country around him with his gray eyes narrowed to glittering slits. His face was bony and darkly weathered. His dark hair had a copper tinge. He wore a flat-crowned black hat, a double-breasted black shirt and black trousers. There was a brown corduroy coat tied behind his saddle. He packed his Smith & Wesson .44 Russian pistols in tied-down holsters.

There were enemies looking for him, and he had no friends anywhere. He kept to himself and there was something about him that kept most people at a distance. Those who ventured closer were usually looking for trouble, and they usually found it.

Two days before at dusk he had stopped at a place called Turley's, a combination store and saloon. Several bearded, rough-garbed men stood at the bar drinking when Graben came in through the swing doors and stopped near the front end of the bar to drink a beer in silence. He did not appear to notice the men but he was aware that they were sizing him up in the back-bar mirror and grinning at one another in a way that spelled trouble. So he finished his beer and went through a doorway into the store to get a sack of grub and a few other things he needed.

When he came back out the five men had left the saloon and were standing outside, near his horse. They were still grinning but there was nothing friendly in their grins. Graben went around them and tied the grub sack to the horn of his saddle in frowning silence, then stepped into the saddle.

"Where'd you get that horse, mister?" one of them said then. It was the youngest of the five, a beardless boy still in his teens.

Graben merely stared at him through cold narrowed eyes and did not bother to answer. A couple of the others took a closer look at him and shifted their feet uncomfortably, perhaps sensing that he was nobody to fool around with. But the kid saw only himself and he liked what he saw.

His voice rose a little. "I'm talkin' to you, mister! I said where did you get that horse?"

Graben still remained silent, watching the boy, watching them all, and it was plain by then that his unexpected silence was getting on their nerves.

The boy's voice was a little shrill as he said, "That there's my horse, mister! He was stole from me a while back!"

Graben merely lifted the reins and started to turn the roan, and as he did so the boy yelled something and went for his gun. A moment later he lay dead in the dirt and Graben's smoking revolver was trained on the others.

"Anybody else think I'm a horse thief?" he asked.

They eyed the gun uneasily and shook their heads.

Then, as Graben backed the horse across the road, still keeping them covered, one of them said, "I shore wouldn't want to be in yore place, mister. That was Tobe Unger's kid brother you killed."

Graben did not know who Tobe Unger was and he did not bother to ask, but he judged that he was somebody to reckon with, or thought he was, and would no doubt be coming after Graben as soon as he heard. And the men who had seen the shooting would be with him. If Graben did not miss his guess, they were already on his trail, and might even circle ahead to set up an ambush.

That was why he studied the old shack with care before riding down the rocky slope toward it. The shack was as weathered and gray as the rocks around it, and looked abandoned. No smoke rose from the rock chimney, there were no horses in the sagging pole corral, and the glassless windows were just empty shadowy holes, like eyes watching him.

For some reason, the place made him uneasy. But he decided he was just jumpy as a result of killing a boy who apparently had a mean, tough brother, and several friends who looked like pirates in western garb.

When he did approach the shack it was by circling down through the rocks and coming up on the shack's blind side, where there were no windows. He might have saved himself the trouble, for when he got inside he found wide cracks between the unchinked logs through which anyone in the one-room shack could have seen him. But there was no one inside the shack and it did not appear that there had been anyone here for some time. The rough plank floor was covered with dust and debris and the stone fireplace was about the same, a good indication that it had not been used recently.

Graben went back outside to the well and drew up the wooden bucket on its frayed, half-rotten rope. There was no water in the bucket. It was half full of sand.

A piercing cackle caused him to drop the bucket and spin around, whipping out a gun. A woman had just emerged from the rocks leading a saddled horse. The sun was directly in Graben's slitted eyes and he could not tell whether the woman's sun-cured face was young or old, whether her hair was gray or sun-bleached blond. But he could tell that she was laughing at him.

"Ain't no water in that well, mister," she said, limping toward him. "Ain't been for years."

Graben's narrow eyes studied the rocks behind her, and seeing this she cackled again and said, "Don't worry, I'm by myself, more's the pity. Nobody wants nothin' to do with Crazy Cora."

She sat down on the ground, tugged off her right boot and rubbed her foot with a callused hand. Graben saw now that she was somewhere in her middle years, but he could not narrow it down much closer than that.

"My horse picked up a limp a piece back," she said with a rueful grin. "Now it looks like I've picked up one, too."

Graben remained silent and she glanced up to study his lean hard face and cold slitted eyes. "I got a place farther back in the hills," she said, hooking a thumb over her shoulder. "Sometimes I come over this way lookin' for strays. Stray men, that is."

She cackled again, but there was no trace of a smile in Graben's eyes. He had not wanted to run into anyone, much less a crazy, man-hunting old woman.

Turning away without a word, he went toward his horse.

"Hey, hold on a minute, mister," she said. "I didn't mean to alarm you. I ain't in the habit of ropin' and brandin' any of the men I see. I just try to find out if they've seen my daughter. She run off with that no-account Tobe Unger three months back and I ain't seen her since."

Graben stopped and turned to look at the woman and he was surprised to see that her faded eyes were damp. Perhaps she was not as crazy as she seemed. "Unger hang ground here much?" he asked.

"Not no more," she said bitterly. "He used to hang around my place all the time till he got my Gibby to run off with him."

"Gibby?"

Crazy Cora tugged off her other boot and massaged that foot also. "I just knowed it was gonna be a boy, and I was gonna name him Gib after his no-account pa what done run off on me. Only it weren't no him, and I named *her* Gibby. Purtiest baby I ever did see and she just got purtier and purtier as she growed up. All I could do to keep men away from her. Wouldn't never allow no men around there on account of her. But that no-account Tobe Unger tricked me, when I should of knowed what he was after. He let on like he was sweet on me, when all he wanted was to use my place for a hideout for him and his gang and to sweet-talk my Gibby behind my back. He ever comes back around, I aim to empty my shotgun at him."

She gestured toward her horse and Graben saw the gun in the saddle scabbard.

"Don't reckon you've seen anything of them?" she asked. "Gibby's a tow-head with light green eyes and the cutest baby face you ever saw. Sometimes it don't seem rightly possible that she could be my girl. She's just seventeen and Tobe Unger's more'n twice that, and a big ugly mean-lookin' rascal. What a girl like her ever saw in him I don't know. Course, in my case there weren't too many men to pick and choose from. But Gibby could of had any man she wanted, and someday the right one would of turned up, and I wouldn't of run him off like I did the others. I kept tellin' her that. Just be patient a while longer, I told her. Don't run off with the first sweet-talkin' rascal that comes along like I did. You'll live to regret it if you do.

"But I never thought to warn her about Tobe Unger, and I sure never thought about him pullin' the wool over my eyes the way he did neither. I knowed he was mean as a snake, but I thought it was all out in the open. He just never seemed to me like the cunnin' type, and when he made such a fuss over my Gibby I just thought it was all in good-natured fun and that he was tryin' to cheer her up 'cause the pore girl always seemed so lonesome without nobody her own age around to talk to. But I guess I should of knowed what he was after all along."

Graben stood by his horse with the reins in his hand, a look of growing impatience in his eyes. He felt sorry for the old woman in a general way, but there was nothing he could do for her, and he did not have time to listen to her troubles. He had his own to worry about, and every moment he remained here increased his danger.

"I haven't seen anyone who looked like your daughter," he said. Then he asked, "Maybe you could tell me where's the nearest water?"

"The nearest water," she said, "is at my place."

Crazy Cora's place turned out to be only a few miles away, and she decided that her horse's feet were in better shape to walk that distance than her own were. En route she explained to Graben that she and "Gib" had squatted on the only sweet waterhole around right after they were married and had hauled logs from mountains thirty miles away to build their one-room cabin, later adding a lean-to kitchen. But in spite of this addition the house turned out to be only a fraction larger than the shack they had just left, and Graben wondered, but did not ask, how they had all managed to crowd into the place when the Unger gang was around. Where had two women and half a dozen men slept? Perhaps the men had slept outside.

The house and waterhole were in a little pocket surrounded by brushy, rocky hills. The area was littered with rocks and boulders that had tumbled down, and Crazy Cora sat down on a nearby rock and watched Graben as he squatted down to fill his canteen while his horse drank beside him. When the woman suddenly let out one of her startling, unexpected cackles, he raised his head and looked at her through cold half-lidded eyes, wondering again if she was as crazy as her nickname implied.

"I was just thinkin' about the look on your face over there when you drawed up that bucket of sand," she said. "What's your name anyway? I know a body ain't supposed to ask, but you don't have to give me your real name. I'd just like to know something to call you when I tell folks about runnin' into you over there and that look on your face."

"Why don't you just make one up for me?" Graben suggested.

She studied him for a moment and then said, "I think I'll call you Graben."

Graben gave her a startled glance. "Why Graben?"

"You remind me of a fellow named Graben who come through here a few months back," she said, again studying his face. "In some ways he looked a lot like you. Tall like you, same color of hair. I think his eyes was more blue than yours. I guess you'd call yours gray, wouldn't you?"

"I would. Some people call them blue."

He pulled his horse back from the water and hung his canteen on the horn. His back to Crazy Cora, he asked, "You happen to catch his first name?"

"Seems like it was Tom," she said. "Yeah, that's what it was, Tom Graben."

Graben had started to tighten his cinch. Now he loosened it again and sat down on a rock not far from Crazy Cora. "That fellow happen to say where he was headed?"

"He never said," Crazy Cora told him. "But it don't matter none, 'cause he never got there, wherever it was."

Graben glanced at her leathery face and bright pale eyes. "What makes you think that?" he asked in the same idle tone as before.

Crazy Cora's own voice dropped to a conspiratorial whisper. "I never meant to tell nobody, but now I don't care who knows about it. They killed him, Tobe and the others did. They thought he was some kind of law snoopin' around, so they killed him."

Graben was prepared for that and there was no change on his bleak weathered face. He showed nothing more than idle curiosity. "Fair fight?"

There was utter scorn in Crazy Cora's pale eyes. "Nah! He looked plumb dangerous, that one did. Them pale cold blue eyes could look right through you and send a chill down your spine. So they didn't take no chances. Shot him down from behind as he started to get on his horse, that fine buckskin Dub Astin still rides. They played poker for his horse and saddle and his guns. Dub got the horse and saddle and Zeke Fossett got the guns."

Frank Graben sat on the rock thinking about what the woman had told him. So Tom was dead, he thought. Tom had been two years older than Frank, and more of a man than he would ever be, but a loner like himself. As boys growing up back in Missouri they had been close, but they had had their differences and had gone their separate ways after their parents died and the farm was sold. Frank had not seen or heard from Tom since, and now he would never see him again.

"Funny thing though," he heard Crazy Cora say. "They took his body back up in the hills yonder and just left him there. A few days later they got to thinkin' maybe they should of hid the body better and went back up there to do the job right. But they never did find him. It was night when they took him up there and left him and it had come a big rain so there wasn't no tracks they could foller back to where they was before. We never could figger out whether they just couldn't find where they left him, or whether somebody had rode by the next day and decided to take him into Rock Crossin' or some-place and bury him decent. We kept expectin' to hear something about it, but we never did, and you can believe we never asked nobody about it."

"No, I guess not," Frank Graben grunted, his eyes unbelievably cold. As cold, Crazy Cora was thinking, as Tom Graben's eyes.

Frank got to his feet and glanced at the unpainted log house. "Anybody else here that night?"

"Mac Radner was here, playin' cards with Tobe and them." She hooked a thumb over her shoulder. "Mac and his two brothers has got them a little place back over here a piece. They call theirselves horse ranchers, but they stole most of them horses. And sometimes they ride with Tobe and the boys if they're wanted or needed."

"Well, I better push on," Graben said, going toward his horse.

Crazy Cora went to her own horse and casually pulled the double barrel shotgun from the scabbard. Graben watched her uneasily, but she made no threatening gesture with the gun and he assumed that she meant to take it inside after he left. "No call to rush off," she said. "I aim to rustle up some chuck here before long, and I might even let you spend the night, if you was lonesome for a little company."

Her sudden cackle made him wince. "I'm not that lonesome," he said, scowling, and stepped into the saddle. "Thanks for the water."

Crazy Cora merely nodded, silent for a change, and watched him turn his horse to ride off. She noticed that he was heading back the way they had come a little earlier, but she did not think anything about it.

She watched him until he was almost out of range, and then she brought up the sawed-off shotgun and fired both barrels at his back, aiming high enough not to hit the horse. Crazy Cora liked horses, but she had no use for men who had no use for her.

She saw the stranger slump forward in the saddle, but somehow he hung on and got the horse into a gallop along the narrow winding valley through which the trail ran.

"He won't git far!" Crazy Cora shrieked, dancing with glee. "Crazy Cora can do it just as good as Tobe and them! I'd go after him, Bess, if you wasn't all gimpy like me!"

Frank Graben did not know how he managed to stay in the saddle, or how far he rode. He was barely conscious most of the time. The horse slowed to a trot and then to a walk, and finally stopped, and he became dimly aware that four rough-looking men sat their horses before him, blocking the trail.

"Well, look who we got here," one of them said in a taunting, vaguely familiar voice. "Tobe is gonna be real pleased when he finds out we done got the man what killed Chip."

"Looks like Crazy Cora already put some buckshot in him," another chuckled.

"Hell, let's finish the bastard and get it over with," said a third.

He could not see their faces clearly, because the light was fading and he could not get his eyes into proper focus for some reason. But now he knew who they were, and he knew they meant to kill him. His hand groped for his gun and found the butt, but the gun seemed to weigh a ton and he did not have the strength to lift it.

Then all four of them were shooting into him and he was falling from the saddle.

A tall man stood up in the rocks on the rough slope above Graben and began firing, the dark long-barreled pistol bucking in his fist. Two of the riders tumbled out of their saddles and the other two turned their horses and spurred away. The tall man in the rocks fired one shot after them and then his gun clicked on an empty chamber.

A minute later Frank Graben found the tall man bending over him.

He peered up into the lean weathered face and cold pale blue eyes of Tom Graben. And that gaunt stubbled face was the last thing Frank Graben saw before he died.

The preceding was from the gritty western novel
The Revenge of Tom Graben

To keep reading, click or go here:
http://amzn.to/1c9lT7s

Excerpt from
Buck Hayden, Mustanger
by Van Holt

Hayden was surprised when he saw smoke curling from the rock chimney. He had figured the old shack below the mesa wall would still be empty. No one had lived there in years. The desert stretching away to the east was too dry and barren for raising anything but rocks, and they grew by themselves. It was no better up on the mesa.

He was even more surprised when he saw the woman standing at the shack door, watching him approach.

When he rode into the dusty yard and drew rein he saw that she was still in her twenties, though at first glance she looked older. Her face was tired and drawn. Her eyes were faded and faint wrinkles and already begun to appear around them. She was tall and slender but rather well developed in all the right places—even her shapeless cotton dress could not hide that fact.

When he touched his flat-crowned black hat, she responded with a slight nod and said, "My husband went to town for supplies, but you're welcome to water your horse and eat here. I'll soon have a bite ready."

"Thanks," he said, stepping down from the saddle. "I'll take the water but pass up the grub. I need to push on."

She silently watched him fill his canteen and water his horse at the half-rotted plank trough. She knew he was wondering about her being here in the old shack, but he asked no questions and hid his curiosity behind a weather-beaten face that was expressionless except for just a hint of wry humor around the thin lips. His eyes were blue but did not seem to have much color until he looked directly at her. Then for a moment the color deepened to a clear sky blue, the change apparently caused by a kind of instinctive alertness. They were not cold eyes, just utterly devoid of warmth.

He seemed a tough, quiet, lonely man, a little remote and unapproachable because he needed no one and preferred to mind his own business. There was no sign of weakness in him, and certainly no softness. He was lean and hard, standing over six feet tall and weighing around a hundred and eighty pounds. He wore a dusty black suit that fit him well, and two guns, one in a cross-draw holster on the left. Both holsters were tied down.

"Do you need two guns?" she asked.

He glanced at her with that brief intensity in his eyes that she had noticed before. A faint, wry smile touched his hard mouth. "They come in handy now and then."

Even as he spoke he looked away, and following his glance, she saw the riders approaching.

Deliberately, he checked his long-barreled revolvers, drawing one at a time, then stood silently watching the riders.

"Do you expect trouble?" she asked uneasily.

He remained standing near his red horse and did not look around at her. He kept his attention on the four riders. "In this country," he said, "it always pays to expect trouble. Speaking for myself, I'm hardly ever disappointed."

"Are you from around here?" she asked.

"I come and go."

The four riders were all young men in their twenties. They made a show of riding boldly into the yard and pulling up in a cloud of dust. Their reckless eyes shifted from Hayden to the woman and back again.

The one in the green shirt said with a sneer, "Well, if it ain't the big bad Buck Hayden himself. What the hell are you doin' here?"

Hayden moved his broad shoulders in a brief shrug. "Passing by."

"Well, you better keep passin'," the rider said, and then turned his eyes on the woman at the door. "Where's your old man?"

"He went to town." Her eyes were uneasy and after a moment she added, "He should be back soon."

"Not unless he left yesterday," the same one snickered, pushing his narrow-brimmed hat back on his curly head. "It'll take him all day in that old wagon. Anyway, it don't matter. You can tell him for us. He better pack up and clear out. This is the last warnin'. He's squattin' on Crown range."

"Since when?" Hayden asked.

The curly head turned back toward him. "Since I said it was," he sneered. "You want to make something of it?"

"Take it easy, Skip," one of the others muttered, watching Hayden with worried eyes.

"Shut up, Pete!" Skip snarled. "Don't nobody tell Skip Leggett what to do!"

"Just Hoffer," Pete grumbled. "And he told us not to cause no trouble where it wasn't necessary."

"What does Hoffer want with this place?" Hayden asked. "Ain't everything west of the mesa enough for him?"

"I reckon he'll be the one to decide that," Skip retorted. He seemed unable to speak in a civil tone. Every word he spoke sounded like a threat or a challenge.

Hayden glanced at the other three. Pete Grimes still seemed anxious to avoid trouble, but Tony Bick and Cal Whitty were grinning maliciously, as if they were enjoying themselves. Hayden considered Tony Bick the most dangerous one of the four. Bick was a tall slender young man with laughing blue eyes and big white teeth. He let Skip Leggett do the talking because that was what Skip was good at, but Bick was ready to do the shooting if there was trouble.

Hayden noticed that Cal Whitty was wearing an extra gun that looked familiar, but he thought it unlikely that it was the one he had in mind. The bottom of Whitty's coat hid both shell belts, and a straggly mustache hid part of his grin.

Hayden's pale eyes turned a shade colder. "You boys better drift along," he said.

Skip Leggett's right hand tensed like a claw over the butt of his holstered gun. His handsome face turned ugly with sneering anger. "Who says?"

Hayden looked deliberately at that threatening hand. "I say," he said quietly.

Pete Grimes spoke quickly. "Remember what Hoffer said, Skip. He said he'd have our hides if we overstepped his orders."

Skip Leggett slowly relaxed and let out the breath he had been holding. His expression remained a sneer, his voice remained sarcastic. "Well, it don't matter whether I kill you now or later, Hayden. But if I wait till Hoffer tells me to do it, he might even give me a bonus."

"You'll earn it," Hayden told him in the same quiet tone.

Skip glared murder at him but said nothing. Pete Grimes looked relieved, Tony Bick and Cal Whitty disappointed. Skip seemed disgusted because his instructions from Hoffer denied him the pleasure of killing Hayden.

He turned his scornful eyes to the woman. "Tell your old man we'll be back, but the next time we'll come shootin'."

She remained silent, hugging herself against the cold wind that the others seemed unaware of. Dust and tumbleweeds drifted across the bleak gray Nevada desert. One tumbleweed rolled up against the water trough and crouched there shivering. The tall man called Hayden stood motionless in the yard, his face like stone, his cold pale eyes never leaving the Crown riders.

Skip Leggett reined his horse around, watching Hayden over his shoulder. "You're the one who better drift along, Hayden," he said. "You better drift right on out of the country. The next time I see you, I'm bettin' I'll have orders from Hoffer to kill you."

"You better bring plenty of help."

Leggett snorted at that and put his horse into a furious gallop back the way they had come. The others were close behind him. Tony Bick threw a look of mock terror back at Hayden, flashing and blinking his eyes wildly. Cal Whitty bent over in his saddle laughing.

"Who is this Hoffer who keep sending men over here?" the woman asked.

Hayden's attention was still on the Crown riders as they followed the dusty trail around a rocky projection of the mesa wall, and he did not answer until they were out of sight. Then a cold smile twisted his lips and he said, "King Hoffer. He came here from Texas a couple years back and pretty soon the people who were already here found out they were squatting on his range. I don't guess they liked it much, but so far nobody's done anything about it. He's either bought out or scared out nearly everyone in the whole country."

"Have you got a place around here?" she asked.

"Not me," he said, stepping into the saddle, all his movements unhurried and effortless. "When I'm around here I stay with Frank Martin and help him hunt wild horses to earn my keep." He smiled faintly. "We used to do that in West Texas before he came here."

The woman looked at him in surprise. "Haven't you heard? He was killed about a week ago. My husband heard about it in town. Some of Hoffer's men went to his place and he tried to run them off with a shotgun, and one of them killed him. That's the story they've been telling anyway."

Hayden's face seemed to turn to stone and a bleak empty look came into his eyes. "When they turned to leave, I thought that was Frank's shotgun and scabbard on Skip Leggett's saddle, and if I'm not mistaken Cal Whitty had his old Starr pistol."

The preceding was from the gritty western novel
Buck Hayden, Mustanger

To keep reading, click or go here:
http://amzn.to/1haTsFq

Excerpt from
The Six-Gun Man

Hanton sat on the long hotel porch, watching dust and tumbleweeds drift along the empty street in the cold wind. Most of the frame and adobe buildings along the street were empty, abandoned.

There hadn't been many people in Ramada five years ago. Now there were only a few left.

He was not sure why he had come back. Curiosity, maybe. He had known there was nothing here for him, and no one who wanted to see him again.

He had stayed here for a while in the fall of 1870. He had been a stranger then. He was still a stranger.

He was a stranger everywhere. Most of the time, he preferred it that way.

It was only when he saw someone like Nora that he wanted to change.

Maybe she was the reason he had come back. If so, he had wasted his time. Nora and her aunt ran the hotel. The older woman had rented him a room and brought the meals he ate in the dining room while Nora kept out of sight in the kitchen. Once when he had seen Nora in the lobby, she had turned her back, pretending not to see him.

He sighed as he thought about her, and glanced down at his old checked suit coat, brown pants, and dusty boots. Under the coat was a cartridge belt, the loops filled with shells for the .44 Smith & Wesson in the Mexican loop holster, which he sometimes wore on his right hip and sometimes over on the left side of his belly for a cross draw.

He stood a little under six feet, which made him taller than most men, but not as tall as some. To his annoyance, most of the men he encountered—especially those he had trouble with—were either taller or stronger than himself, or both. Where were the small weak men when he needed them?

The smelly man at the livery stable down the street, though old, was big and strong. When Dan Hanton was giving instructions for the care of his horse, the old man had got up in his face and said, "I only been takin' care of horses close to fifty years now. Maybe you'd like to take yours somewhere else."

Hanton had glanced up the deserted street. "Is there another stable in this town?"

"You know there ain't. I remember you. You're that saddle bum who was here several years ago. Why did you come back?"

"Just passing through."

"That's what you said the last time. But you hung around for over a month."

"Three weeks."

"It seemed longer."

The old liveryman's name was Gandy Sweet. He had a wide face made wider still by a gray-streaked black beard that stuck out in every direction. He wore a beat-up old hat and a filthy black coat.

"Horse looks in good shape," he said, glancing at Hanton's roan gelding. "If I was you, I'd keep movin'. There's some fellers here now who don't want no strangers hangin' around."

Hanton turned his head and studied the silent old buildings along Ramada's only street. Some of the buildings were boarded up. Most of them looked abandoned. Tall dead weeds and brush had grown up through the rotting plank porches of several of the buildings.

"It don't look to me like nobody's here," he said.

"They stay out at Pop Lovett's ranch part of the time."

"Lovett's store still open?"

"Part of the time. Pop stays out at his ranch more now. He tried to get his daughter Helen to run the store for him, but she'd rather be a cowgirl. Pop's out at his ranch now, but he'll most likely be back before the stage comes through around noon tomorrow, in case the passengers want to buy something."

"The hotel still open?"

"So far. I don't know how much longer Ruth will be able to keep it open, the way things is goin'. Too bad. Ruth's a mighty fine woman. And Nora seems almost like her own daughter instead of her niece." He gave Hanton a hard look. "You keep away from her, you hear? And if you're gonna put up at the Price Hotel, I want you to pay Ruth in advance, in case something happens to you."

"What could happen to me?"

A malicious smile twisted Sweet's wide flat mouth. "I figure you'll soon be dead."

He turned and led Hanton's roan into the stable.

That conversation had taken place yesterday morning. Now it was almost noon of the day that the westbound stage was supposed to come through town. It would stop at the hotel and the driver and the shotgun guard and any passengers would eat their dinner in the hotel dining room while Gandy Sweet changed the horses. He would eat his dinner after the stage left.

The hotel was on the south side of the street, on a scarcely perceptible elevation near the center of town. A small abandoned frame building stood between the hotel and Pop Lovett's store. There were two more abandoned buildings between the store and the livery stable.

Apparently all the buildings on the far side of the street were abandoned except a saloon and the house next to it, where the saloonkeeper lived. Since Hanton did not drink, he had not been in the saloon.

He looked along the street toward the rough, broken hills east of town. Out there somewhere, a few miles to the south of the stage road, was the Lovett ranch. There was so little grass and water in that country, it was said that about a hundred acres were needed for each cow. No wonder the Lovett ranch was the only one in over a hundred dry miles.

Hanton had learned how to survive in such country and had even come to prefer it, because there were fewer people and he wanted to be alone. But at times he missed the forests and farms of Alabama, where he had spent the first sixteen years of his life, before the Civil War.

He had grown up on a small farm a few miles from a crossroads store. There was no town in thirty miles. There were no large plantations in that part of the country, and only a few blacks. Most of the people in the area were fiercely independent hill folks. When the war started, they refused to fight to protect the large plantations in the Tennessee River Valley and the Black Belt, or the slave property on those plantations. The Hantons had no slaves and did not hold with slavery. But they considered the South their country and believed it was their duty to do what they could to repel the Yankee invasion.

Dan had been the youngest of four children. The oldest was Maude. She was fifteen years older than Dan but still unmarried when the war started. In between them were two boys, Matt and Sam. Matt, only a year younger than Maude, had married a widow with two little girls. The mother died just before the war started, and she had no folks. The girls were then eight and ten.

"I don't see how I can go," Matt said, looking somber and depressed.

"I figure there'll be plenty of fightin' around here, the way some folks are talkin'," Sam said.

"Just let them talk," Dan said. "You and Matt stay here and make a crop. I'll go and help them fight the Yankees. I figure it'll be over by fall."

He had returned four years later and found Maude putting flowers on two fresh graves. Matt's name was carved on one of the plain wooden markers and Samuel's on the other.

"What happened?" Dan asked from the saddle of his worn-out old horse.

Maude wore a patched, faded old dress and looked worn out herself. She said in a tired, hopeless voice, "You know how Matt and Sam was. Everybody else around here was Unionists, and Matt and Sam let them know what they thought of them. Matt wouldn't let Rose and June have anything to do with Nib and Tuck Moody. Said them girls was too young to have anything to do with wild boys who was always in some kind of trouble. But Nib and Tuck said it was because they was Unionists. They come by here late last Tuesday when it was startin' to get dark and found Matt and Sam standin' out in the yard talkin'. Neither Matt nor Sam had a gun, but Nib and Tuck had brought their pistols with them. I was in the kitchen gettin' supper ready and I don't know what was said. The first thing I heard was shootin' and when I got outside I saw Matt and Sam layin' on the ground and Nib and Tuck Moody was ridin' off with Rose and June up on the horses behind them. The girls never even come back for the funeral, such as it was. The truth is, I had to bury Matt and Sam right by myself. The people around here who would have helped were afraid they'd get the Moodys mad at them. It's been like that around here ever since the war started, and even before."

Dan Hanton looked at this plain, manlike sister of his. She was thirty-five and looked closer to fifty. He had never seen her in a pretty dress or a new one. She always wore the old clothes that had belonged to her dead mother. Just thinking about her sad life filled him with an almost unbearable feeling of pity. And there was nothing he could do for her. He couldn't stay here now without bringing more trouble down on her.

As if reading his mind, she said, "I don't know what I'll do, now that Matt and Sam are dead."

"I know what I'll do," Dan said, checking the loads in his Navy Colt.

Maude looked at him in alarm. "There's been enough killin' already."

Dan Hanton's eyes were hard, merciless. "Too much. But the wrong people got killed. Matt and Sam should have been wearing their guns and made sure the right people got killed."

At that moment Nib and Tuck Moody came riding along the road and turned into the yard. Each had a pistol stuck in his waistband. Even in their battered old hats and patched homespun clothes, they were good-looking boys, with shaggy blond hair and blue eyes. Dan watched them warily and reluctantly holstered his gun.

Nib gave Dan a mean look and said, "I figured the Yankees had killed you by now. We laughed every time we heard about them chasin' you Rebs."

"It wasn't always them chasing us. Sometimes we did the chasing."

"They won. That's what counts." Nib turned his scornful attention to Maude. "We come to git Rose and June. Tell them there ain't no use hidin' in the house. We'll just come in atter them."

Maude blinked in surprise. "They ain't here. The last time I saw them, they was ridin' off with you and Tuck."

"They run off. We figured they'd come back home."

"I ain't seen them."

"I think you're lyin'. Tuck, take a look in the house."

"Tuck better stay out of the house," Dan said.

Maude moved in long strides to place herself between Dan and the Moody boys. "Just leave them alone, Dan. The Lord will punish them, in His own good time."

Nib grinned with is big white teeth. "He prob'ly will, but we aim to have us a lot of fun first. Look in the house, Tuck, and make sure they ain't hidin' under the bed or in the closet. Dan won't bother you. He always was yaller. Lafe said he prob'ly spent the war runnin' from the Yankees and hidin' from them."

"How did Lafe spend the war?"

"Him and Tobe and the Fink boys spent most of it robbin' Rebs and raidin' plantations in the Tennessee Valley. But they was so bad even the Yankee soldiers started lookin' for them and they had to clear out. Said they was goin' out west. Rose and June said we should go out there and find them, 'cause you'd be comin' back soon and would want them to come back home."

"Rose and June are just little girls, for Christ's sake."

"Wait till you see them. Rose looks almost like a grown woman. June ain't quite thirteen, but she's already stickin' out in all the right places. And she'll do anything to prove she's just as wild as Rose."

"It's true," Maude said. "Both of them girls went wild after they started sneakin' out to meet Nib and Tuck in the woods. Matt couldn't do anything with them. He hated to whup them."

"We woulda killed him if he had," Nib said.

"You killed him and Sam anyway," Dan said bitterly. "And Maude said they weren't armed."

"Bein' armed won't do you no good," Nib said. "You shouldn't have put that Navy Colt back in the holster when you saw us comin'. Tuck, you're a little quicker than me, 'cause you practice all the time. Kill the bastard, or he'll kill us. I can see it in his eyes."

"No!" Maude screamed as Tuck Moody's right hand slapped the butt of his gun. She ran up to Tuck's horse and reached up to jerk the gun out of his hand. The gun was pointed at her when it roared, but she held onto the barrel and pulled the cussing boy out of the saddle as she fell. Tuck hit the ground beside her and wrenched his gun free a split second before Dan put a bullet between his eyes.

Dan turned his gun on Nib as Nib frantically went for his own gun. Dan shot him off his horse and shot him again as he lay on the ground, still trying to fight.

Maude was dead, her shocked eyes wide open. Dan buried her in a shallow grave near the graves of Matt and his wife, Sam and their parents. Dan was the only one left, besides the two girls who had disappeared. Dan had to disappear too. He had left Alabama and never gone back. He was the only one who knew for sure who had killed Nib and Tuck Moody.

Dan had never tried to find Rose and June, who would be grown women in their twenties now, if they were still alive. In his heart he had disowned them, though he guessed Nib and Tuck Moody had led them astray before they were old enough to make the right decisions.

Some girls were too easily led astray.

To keep reading, click or go here
http://amzn.to/1itBSM0

More hellbound gunslinging westerns by Van Holt:

A Few Dead Men
http://amzn.to/18Xu7ic

Blood in the Hills
http://amzn.to/16jWNvB

Brandon's Law
http://amzn.to/1fijGsy

Buck Haden, Mustanger
http://amzn.to/1haTsFq

Curly Bill and Ringo

http://amzn.to/Z6AhSH

Dead Man Riding
http://amzn.to/1aknrFD

Dead Man's Trail
http://amzn.to/ZcPJ47

Death in Black Holsters
http://amzn.to/1aHxGcv

Dynamite Riders
http://amzn.to/ZyhHmg

Hellbound Express
http://amzn.to/11i3NcY

Hunt the Killers Down
http://amzn.to/Z7UHjD

Maben
http://amzn.to/1judfzK

Rebel With A Gun
http://amzn.to/1apARDN

Riding for Revenge
http://amzn.to/13gLILz

Rubeck's Raiders
http://amzn.to/14CDxwU

Shiloh Stark
http://amzn.to/12ZJxcV

Shoot to Kill
http://amzn.to/18zA1qm

Six-Gun Solution
http://amzn.to/10t3H3N

Six-Gun Serenade
http://amzn.to/164cS7t

Six-Gun Man
http://amzn.to/1itBSM0

Six-Gun Showdown
http://amzn.to/1eDt8Fi

Son of a Gunfighter
http://amzn.to/17QAzSp

The Antrim Guns
http://amzn.to/132I7jr

The Bounty Hunters

http://amzn.to/10gJQ6C

The Bushwhackers
http://amzn.to/13ln4JO

The Fortune Hunters
http://amzn.to/11i3VsO

The Gundowners
(formerly So, Long Stranger)
http://amzn.to/16c0I2J

The Gundown Trail
http://amzn.to/1g1jDNs

The Hellbound Man
http://amzn.to/1fTATJy

The Hell Riders
http://amzn.to/1haTsFq

The Last of the Fighting Farrells
http://amzn.to/Z6AyVI

The Long Trail
http://amzn.to/137P9c8

The Man Called Bowdry
http://amzn.to/14LjpJa

The Return of Frank Graben
http://amzn.to/1eeiDpk

The Revenge of Sam Graben
http://amzn.to/1c9lT7s

The Six-Gunner
http://amzn.to/1pF9mOO

The Return of the Six-Gunner
Coming Soon!

The Stranger From Hell
http://amzn.to/12qVVqd

The Vultures
http://amzn.to/12bjeGl

Wild Country
http://amzn.to/147xUDq

Wild Desert Rose
http://amzn.to/XH7Y27

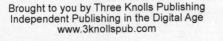
Brought to you by Three Knolls Publishing
Independent Publishing in the Digital Age
www.3knollspub.com

About the Author:

Van Holt wrote his first western when he was in high school and sent it to a literary agent, who soon returned it, saying it was too long but he would try to sell it if Holt would cut out 16,000 words. Young Holt couldn't bear to cut out any of his perfect western, so he threw it away and started writing another one.

A draft notice interrupted his plans to become the next Zane Grey or Louis L'Amour. A tour of duty as an MP stationed in South Korea was pretty much the usual MP stuff except for the time he nabbed a North Korean spy and had to talk the dimwitted desk sergeant out of letting the guy go. A briefcase stuffed with drawings of U.S. aircraft and the like only caused the overstuffed lifer behind the counter to rub his fat face, blink his bewildered eyes, and start eating a big candy bar to console himself. Imagine Van Holt's surprise a few days later when he heard that same dumb sergeant telling a group of new admirers how he himself had caught the famous spy one day when he was on his way to the mess hall.

Holt says there hasn't been too much excitement since he got out of the army, unless you count the time he was attacked by two mean young punks and shot one of them in the big toe. Holt believes what we need is punk control, not gun control.

After traveling all over the West and Southwest in an aging Pontiac, Van Holt got tired of traveling the day he rolled into Tucson and he has been there ever since, still dreaming of becoming the next Zane Grey or Louis L'Amour when he grows up. Or maybe the next great mystery writer. He likes to write mysteries when he's not too busy writing westerns or eating Twinkies.

WARNING: Reading a Van Holt western may make you want to get on a horse and hunt some bad guys down in the Old West. Of course, the easiest and most enjoyable way to do it is vicariously – by reading another Van Holt western.

Van Holt writes westerns the way they were meant to be written.

Printed in Great Britain
by Amazon.co.uk, Ltd.,
Marston Gate.